THE
MUSKIE HOOK

PETER ZACHARY COHEN

THE
MUSKIE HOOK

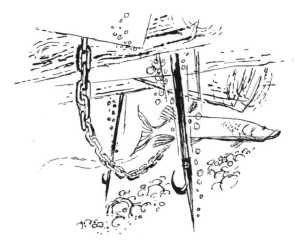

drawings by Tom O'Sullivan

ATHENEUM   1969   NEW YORK

FOR JAY

because he helped with the fishing

& the writing

THE
MUSKIE HOOK

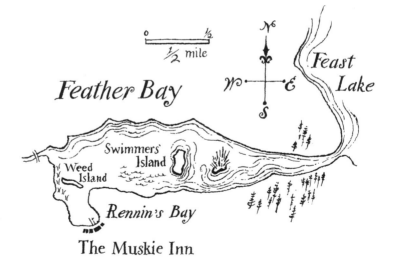

Feather Bay

Feast Lake

N S E W

0 ½
½ mile

Swimmers Island

Weed Island

Rennin's Bay

The Muskie Inn

1

AARON RENNIN lived at the Muskie Inn.

There he met a lot of people who traveled long distances and spent a lot of money to come to fish for the muskellunge, and usually his father or his brother would guide them. When there was no guiding, his father or his brother would go out fishing anyway, and more and more his father had been taking Aaron with him. Then usually his mother would go along, too.

"Why don't we go up into the woods today for a change," Aaron would say. "There's some bass lakes up there, and we could look around and come home with a mess of fish, too."

"Just as soon as you're old enough and strong enough, we'll get you a guide boat of your own," his father would promise.

"Nils Carlson's dad's got a new horse to snake logs out of the boggy places," Aaron would say. "It's big as an elephant. It's even got a nose like one. You ought to see it."

"You never know what a muskie's going to do or how you'll have to play one; so the more experience you get now, the better off you'll be," his father would say, as if he hadn't heard a word.

So Aaron would go out in the boat and cast his bait in and out all day, or sometimes they would just sit and troll their baits behind them endlessly. He'd been going out like that ever since he was five. Six times he'd seen muskies explode completely out of the water, big as fence posts, their bodies shimmering dark and silver; they had danced on their tails and then plunged down with their back fins glowing blood-red just before they disappeared. Aaron had seen four of those muskies brought into the boat. That was not many fish for seven years.

He preferred the few times each year when, by talking steadily about it, he'd gotten to ride the school bus through all of its hour-long trip, into the early darkness of the northern winter. Then he had spent the weekend with Nils, and Nils' dad had always let the two of them go with him for a while around the timber camp, and he'd given them steel helmets to wear, saying, "There's always something going on around here, so you've got to be careful."

Aaron had seen the tall trees come crashing down, smashing the brush beneath, and the sunlight shining down where it had not really been for years. He had smelled the fresh wood and the gouged up dirt, and watched the men moving about with horses and saws and axes and chains and tractors and trucks. Afterward he had scrambled over the brush and wandered around the new clearings, excited by all the work they had done. Always there would be another log truck standing ready to head for town, loaded.

Few boats ever came back loaded to the docks of the Muskie Inn.

Aaron had seen almost every kind of equipment taken in the boats. Most people brought short casting rods that bent like whips; but some brought long thin rods, usually handiest amongst the lily pads for fish no bigger than bass; some people carried the thick heavy rods meant for ocean fishing; and a few insisted on using bamboo poles as stiff and stout as pine saplings.

They worked minnows for bait, or wooden plugs painted to resemble small fish, or metal spoons, or bundles of animal hair, or contraptions that spun and gurgled. They tied them onto their lines with metal leaders, because muskies had teeth like timber saws. But nothing did much good, not even the big medicine bag that the quiet little druggist brought every year from Tennessee. His name was Mr. Carner, and his bag was full of baits. He was coming again in

6

July, even though for eleven straight years he'd never caught a single muskie.

"Why don't you go somewhere else?" Aaron had finally asked him.

"I've fished here so long, I'm bound to catch one soon," he'd said. "I can't afford to start all over in a new place."

Mr. Grilfurth, the banker from Oklahoma, had been coming to the Inn every year since before Aaron was born—for fifteen years—and he'd caught eleven muskies, mostly with spoons. But he could stay for a whole month in the fall when the water was low and the natural food in the bays was scarce. He fished all of every possible day. His skin grew sandpapery, for the fall days could be as raw as the springtime. The man had fished, Aaron had noted, feeling embarrassed, over four hundred days for nothing.

"But you haven't counted the five times they've broken my line, and the twenty-two times I've seen them charge my bait. Eighteen times they've struck at my bait and missed." Mr. Grilfurth had laughed, as he spoke.

One man with thick gray hair had said he'd saved for three years to come fish muskies for two weeks. Aaron could remember him standing on the lawn of the Inn and crying plainly in the lamplight after his last day darkened and he'd had to come in without a catch. Other people had gotten angry and not returned. Then new people always came, wanting to try.

But Aaron was more and more uncomfortable living where grown men cried, or bragged of fights they had lost. And where it didn't seem to bother his father or his brother to go out day after day and come back empty and take pay for finding nothing.

"The muskie is king," his father would say, "and a king doesn't come to town very often."

So in the light of most dawns, from thaw in May until freeze in November, Aaron would watch the boats move apart from the docks, and their outboard motors start roaring and kicking up waves so strongly that the people in them seemed to sink shoulder-deep in the water itself as they sped away.

Then—when there was no school—he would mow all around the Inn, and the grass would look greener and neater when he was done.

Or he would feed the minnows in the tank, and they would always come darting eagerly for the food he tossed them. Or he would swab the boats that weren't being used, or haul away the garbage from the lodge and the six cabins; and when he was done, the whole Inn would seem better and fresher because of him, even though the glow of the sky would be getting gray.

Then one or two loons would always be sounding their evening yodels as he began waiting. Until all the boats were in, he waited for the distant mutterings of a motor, if the wind were right; and if it weren't, he watched for the first steady movements at the mouth of the channel that lay across the small body of water called Rennin's Bay.

He would wait next to an old school bell that hung now from three crossed poles; and if any boat as it emerged from the channel was flying a small red flag, Aaron would leap to the rope and make the bell clang. The clanging would send the loons flapping along the water and into the sky, and no doubt it startled any deer in the pine woods behind him, and certainly it brought people gathering down at the dock to welcome home the muskie-catcher like a conquering hero.

Perhaps six or eight times each year he was able to clang the bell. Every other evening the boats glided in silently except for the churglings of the big outboard motors. The people would be sitting stiff and erect. In the dim twilight their shapes were like old propped-up toothpaste tubes with all the excitement of the morning departure squeezed out.

They would stare quietly back at anyone who was there to meet them. They wouldn't notice any freshness he'd brought to the boats or lawn. They scarcely noticed the mosquitoes. They would simply climb

9

out and stand around awkwardly, with nothing to hold but their fishing tackle, which was thin and useless then. Finally they might start talking in low, short tones, and begin to make laughs that would rattle around the Inn for the rest of the evening, without any happiness in them.

In the roughest weather the people stayed near the lodge all day and laughed more easily, and hopefully. And they were all very pleasant to each other, it seemed, so that the spirits that might be watching their behavior would not deny them good luck later. Around the Inn, Aaron usually liked the stormy days —the days when no boats went out—better.

2

LIGHTNING SNAPPED and flashed just as Aaron got in through the doorway; immediately thunder, loud and sharp, echoed away. For a moment he heard the windows in the main lodge-room shaking. The hall calendar stayed hanging solidly beside the closet.

In a fresh silence the drumming of the rain outside continued.

Then a man's voice from the lodge-room exclaimed, "Wow!"

Another said, "Gentlemen, that was a pole-splitter."

Aaron recognized both voices, and knew there ought to be a third. He was drenched from his long run in from the school bus, and he began slowly unpeeling and putting away his dripping rainclothes. The calendar kept telling him with black numbers that there were only two weeks left of school, and he was still carrying his unanswered invitation around in his head.

Nils' dad had said it would be fine if he came to live at the timber camp this summer, right after school was out. That way he'd have time to learn how to cruise the woods to find trees that were right for cutting. He'd get to do some of the trimming. But his father still said he couldn't go.

"D'ya suppose that thunder's got their heads buried in the mud yet, Brig?" the first man's voice spoke again, and chuckled.

"A muskie's no catfish!" That was his father—Brig —quick and sharp as the lightning whenever anyone said anything the least bit bad about muskies. "When a muskie's hungry, no sky thunder's going to stop him."

"Funny then, how that sky thunder never lets them get hungry," said the first man's voice teasingly.

"It stuns the small fish, maybe, so they're easy caught. Then the muskies don't get hungry," Aaron heard his brother, Roger, say.

"I would expect the storm riles the water so they can't see," said the second voice—a deep, very sure-sounding voice.

"That would make them hungrier, and our chances tomorrow all the better," the third man's voice finally sounded, cheerily.

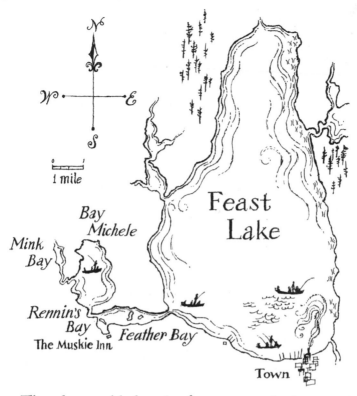

Thunder rumbled again, from across the bay.

"You can't say 'never' about muskies. Just once in a while you can get reckless and say 'maybe'," his father said good-naturedly, and the men all chuckled quietly, in different tones.

Down to dry clothes, Aaron went on into the lodge-room. Roger saw him in the doorway and immediately called at him, "Hey, Books, don't they teach you in school how come muskies don't like to bite after a storm?"

"Who cares?" Aaron spoke back sharp and quick, like his father had, and all the men looked up. Through another fresh silence in the room the rain drumming outside kept going. He thought: *But I didn't mean to say it that way. I really didn't mean to say it at all. It won't help me a bit!*

But he had just gotten off the school bus, was all; he'd had to watch it go on without him again to the timber camps. He still couldn't go there this summer. And his feelings had burst out here.

Tight-lipped, he kept on walking through the lodge-room.

His father came into his bedroom that evening. The rain outside had become a drizzle, though new thunder seemed to be booming distantly.

"Now," his father said, "what was that remark about?"

"What remark?" said Aaron, trying to give himself a moment more to think.

"About not caring why muskies are usually harder to catch after a storm," his father said, giving him time to think, but not letting the subject stray.

Aaron took a deep breath.

He said, "You know what it's about. It's no fun."

"What isn't?" said his father.

"Fishing," said Aaron. And then in a light voice: "Muskies."

His father coughed and stuttered abruptly. And then he just snorted and stared down at Aaron and jammed his hands in his pockets. "What's no fun?" he answered loudly. "Catching muskies isn't fun?"

"No! I mean *yes*," said Aaron. "But you never catch them."

"Never catch them!"

"No! I mean—it's only maybe eight a year. It's—it's—like going every day to get an ice cream and only getting one eight times a year! Like I've told you!"

Aaron had begun talking loudly, too, nearly shouting. "It hurts. It's not fun," he said.

"Fun kind of depends." His father wasn't calming either. "You rather go digging all day in a strip mine?"

"No," said Aaron.

"Then *what* is fun to you?"

Aaron took a deeper breath. He started to say, *You know*. But he answered straight off: "Logging."

He saw his father take a breath. He saw the muscles of his father's cheek clench and ripple as he knew they would.

"Nils Carlson," his father growled.

"Yes," said Aaron.

"And still Turtle County?"

"Yes," said Aaron.

"And moving off to Montana some day?"

"Yes," said Aaron.

15

"You and the money-eyes!" groaned his father. "They knock down anything for a dime. And you want to chase after them!"

Aaron twisted inside himself but couldn't hold back what he felt. "They give logs for their money," he said. "They don't bring people back with nothing. Guiding feels like cheating."

His father's cheeks clenched and rippled quickly again.

"Nils Carlson tells you I'm cheating?"

"No," said Aaron.

"You think I'm cheating? You think my guests keep coming because they think I'm cheating?"

"I don't know why they keep coming."

"What else did Nils Carlson tell you?"

"We talk about logging."

"And you want to be a logger. You hear the loons talk every day, too. How come you don't want to be a loon?"

"I don't know," said Aaron. "I never thought about it. I guess for the same reason you don't want to be a logger."

His father's eyes glared at him.

"Listen," said his father. "If a man can do one thing good, he can do another. When you get big enough, we'll start you guiding. When you get good at that and still want to log, I'll help you go. Then you'll be able to handle anything you hook."

"I already keep the Inn mowed and cleaned and patched, don't I?" said Aaron. "I always get those things done good, don't I?"

"Yes," said his father. "If you didn't, I wouldn't have come to talk about it."

3

LONG. THICK. *Side stripes blending with the wavy shadows coming down from the surface, the muskie began drifting back into a low patch of early weeds. He was alert, restless, uncomfortable—but he moved slowly and calmly. He knew his way and had heard many thunders before. He could see the shimmer of a few smaller fish among the weeds. They sparkled away from him in sharper turns than he could make. He settled at the edge of the weeds. He didn't like the thunder, but had never found it; there was never anything to chase and strike at. He would wait.*

He sensed the flickers of the lightning getting brighter. The vibrations of thunder came harder. He began to hear again the chatter of rain striking the water's surface.

He had to wait. He lay floating. The two pairs of

18

fins on his belly, so small they looked like accidental slivers, were scarcely fanning. His sharply forked tail and the big top and bottom fins near it kept spreading out and folding slowly like dark sails.

Again the wide flashing above him; the thunder shook right after it. Again. Brighter and harder.

He didn't like it. He was restless. He grew nervous. A movement near him: he swirled and struck wide-mouthed—then shook viciously, writhed end over, and sped through the weeds letting them clog and snag from his teeth the ragged ends of an old and sunken bird's nest.

Then he returned to the low edge of the weeds, restless, waiting.

4

NEXT MORNING the rain was gone, but heavy clouds remained, and beneath the clouds a wind was coming swiftly out of the North; and so the water of Rennin's Bay looked black and was charging at the shore in hard, jumpy waves that tossed up thin streaks of white foam like cold sweat.

From out on the water, and in through the glass of the shut window, a loon's yodel sounded, like a musical shriek of distress. Aaron had heard many such cries before and doubted that the loon was in trouble. Anyway what could be done? How could he find the thin, black-and-white head among all the black-and-white water?

But near the weeds along the eastern edge of the bay he could see a group of ducks bobbing up and down. Boats as small as the ducks would have been sunk in a moment. The ducks rode about in the cold wind and rough water as easily as they seemed to do on a quiet summer day.

Aaron watched the ducks for a long time, while he should have been dressing and getting ready for school. His father had once told him that snapping turtles sometimes swam from beneath and snatched at a floating duck to drag it down, and that sometimes muskies or big northern pike rose to strike at them. Since then he often watched ducks, always a little breathlessly, and always a little longer than he meant to. He didn't wish the ducks any harm, but as long as one or two were bound to get caught, he wanted a chance to see how it happened.

The chance had never yet come; and now with another feeling of wasted hope, he started to turn away. It was as he drew his glance inward that he noticed the empty space along the docks. A guide boat was gone. For several seconds he kept staring to make sure the emptiness wasn't just a trick of his eyes, or of a drop of blown spray upon his window. Then he quickly dressed.

"Yes, it's the same three men Dad's been with all week," his mother answered when he reached the kitchen. "They have to go home Sunday, and they want all the fishing they can get."

"Who can fish in an open boat in those waves? They'll spend all their time keeping from getting swamped. They said they couldn't catch muskie after a storm anyway."

"I'm sure your father must know what he's doing," his mother said. Then: "Now you eat and get, so you don't have to chase that bus all the way to town. I've got to help Roger pack so *he* can get going."

"Where's Rog going?"

"To the boat show in Minneapolis this weekend, remember?"

"Another one?"

"He wants a certain kind of boat. Now you keep moving. See that clock?"

"I see," said Aaron. Hurriedly he finished eating, threw on his coat and grabbed up his books. The moment he stepped outside, the wind, rushing raw and damp through the northern springtime, tried to tear everything away from him. He could hear the splashing and spraying of the bay more sharply. He ducked his head and hurried with the weather along the drive that led across the big lawn and then curved into a short arm of the forest.

The moment he got there the wind let go of him. It couldn't twist and follow among the trees, though Aaron could hear it whirring through the upper branches; the whirring drowned out the noises of the bay. Without the wind, in spite of the extra shadiness, it felt warm.

Around his feet on the sandy drive, neatly superimposed on the rain-spatter marks, were the scattered footprints of the mice and skunks and raccoons, and a single deer, that had crossed during the night after the rain had stopped. As always, Aaron went slowly and quietly through the narrow forest, for there might be a raccoon or the deer lingering somewhere.

He saw a rabbit hunched almost invisibly against the road. Aaron stopped, and then moved softly closer among the edge of berry bushes. The rabbit leaped into the brush, too, and Aaron laughed at the puff of sand kicked up behind it that looked for a moment as if the rabbit were still there. He could have tracked it, but there was no time.

There were always deer to track, for the fun of it, through the timber thickets. He and Nils had gone out there on Sundays and had never failed to see them go in white-tailed leaps through the forest. And almost every time, he'd had grouse drum up from right by his feet and then stop on the first limb, live statues holding so still and close that every color of every feather showed. A man with only a slingshot would never have to starve. He and Nils always kept ready to yell and howl like Indians to drive any bear away; they'd been told that when a bear ran scared, he left a whole new road through the woods—

But there were too many people around the bay shores for there to be much game there.

When he came out of the woods, the school bus

was already in sight, slowing up to stop by the Muskie Inn's mailbox. In those few seconds before its motor was rumbling impatiently in front of him, it occurred to Aaron to wonder how come Roger got to go off to so many boat sales.

He couldn't wonder long.

The moment he got to the back of the heated, jiggling school bus, Aaron found himself fighting for the seat Nils Carlson had been saving him.

Kent Towle tried to snatch loose his schoolbooks. Wes Goranson slid across the aisle into the seat beside Nils, and Nils started shoving him back. Aaron swung his books to safety beneath another seat and tried to grab Wes's arm, but got banged hard in the ribs by a seat-back as Kent pushed him.

He knew no one cared whether he got into the seat or not, that this was just a game of "keep-away," to see how big a fight they could stir up before Nate Jennerson stopped the bus and came back after them.

But this morning Aaron didn't want to be bothered with games. His meeting with his father last night made it necessary he talk with Nils again right away. The sharp blow in his ribs knocked away his patience.

He struck fiercely with the stiff edge of his hand at Kent Towle's shoulder; Kent yelped and jumped back. Aaron turned and yanked Wes from the seat as

Nils pushed; then his left foot was jerked up off the floor by Kent's hands and, off balance, Aaron banged his ribs against the seat-back again. He grabbed hold of the seat-back and shook and stomped his foot free and started to shove his way past Kent—but the suddenly slowing bus sent them all sprawling.

For the rest of the trip Aaron sat up front beside six-year-old Karen Dingling. As he stared at the back of Nate Jennerson's head, he thought worriedly of how difficult it was to accomplish anything.

His classes were endless. Through the windows he could see the wide sweep of water where Feast Lake came from an endless way off, to the very edge of town. Its rough, dark waves had begun rolling more smoothly, becoming bluer—and sometimes lightly greenish—as the cloudiness began to go away. And in front of the waves he could see the huge smoking anthill that was the sawdust burner of the sawmill along the shore.

He kept watching for the logging trucks coming in. They came in from the same road his school bus had taken, in from beyond where the road veered away from the bays, in from where dirt and sand roads went shadily and silently and mysteriously on into the vast forests of Turtle County. He'd been a short ways on some of those roads when he visited Nils, and he'd seen the big trucks go traveling by.

Now from time to time he could watch them dumping their log-bolts, making stormy splashes in the holding pond where the bolts would be floated into position for the mill.

Then the empty trucks would start back: to where the men and saws and axes were busily roaring and shouting and climbing and swinging away at the giant forest. *I will, too!* Aaron thought. *But you've got to know so much to get started.*

It'd be possible with Nils. We'll get paid this summer, five cents a stick for stripping bark off the thin poles being shipped for pulp, and we'll learn how to measure the trees to be cut. That way we'll get to work next summer, too, and before we're out of school we'll know how to cut them so they fall just right. We'll get good enough to cut thirty trees a day, and we'll come to town regularly, loaded full each time.

Then we'll be off to Montana, and learn how to log on the steep mountainsides. Then we'll be ready for Oregon and California, where the trees are two hundred feet high.

Then Alaska . . .

Then Mexico . . .

"Aaron Rennin!" His teacher's voice caught his attention. "If you don't pay attention to these algebra problems now, you'll be helpless when you grow up. Think of your future, Aaron."

5

HE DIDN'T GET to talk with Nils until lunchtime, and then not again till they got back on the bus. They sat and watched Nate Jennerson glancing often up into the big mirror that showed him the whole back of the bus. Wes Goranson and Kent Towle were making faces toward the mirror.

"Your dad's just like old Jennerson," Nils said. "Always getting in the way of things. Maybe if your dad drove a school bus, he wouldn't be so dead set on having you around all the time."

"You'd think he'd let me go away for one summer. You'd think he'd let me do something else for a change," Aaron said, "besides waiting around to pull a bell six times all year. You'd think he'd let me go *learn* something."

"You'll need experience if we're going to go logging," Nils said. "You'll just have to keep after him."

"That just makes him mad."

"Well, maybe you'll make him just mad enough to send you off. But don't let him start you guiding."

"What's the difference?"

"You'll be just like Nate. My dad told me he used to ride to school with Nate's dad driving. Then one year Nate's dad stayed home for the first day of hunting season, and Nate drove that day, and Nate's been driving ever since. So if you start guiding, you'll never get loose; you'll never come logging, I'll bet you."

"Not me. Don't worry about that," said Aaron. "I'll try him again tonight."

"And stick with your garbage-hauling."

"Maybe he'll let me haul it up to your place."

Nils laughed. "Tell him we're hungry. Starving. We'll eat anything."

Aaron laughed, too; then stopped. His laughing felt hollow. "Well, I hope I get to see you before Monday—"

When the bus had stopped, and gone, Aaron started back through the shady reach of the forest and pretended he was going along deep in the forest, marking timber for logging. Then he came out onto the big lawn. The wind had dropped, and deep blue afternoon sky was all around a few leftover clouds; the bay was quieting. It would be a good weekend for going up to Turtle County.

He went on across the lawn, trying to feel as happy and hopeful as he could, and went into the lodge-room, and found the same three men seated there.

Automatically the oddness struck him. The weather was calming, yet they were in here. *They've caught a big one!* he started to think, but he knew just as quickly, could tell by the dull atmosphere, that they hadn't.

"Your father took sick in the boat, right after noon," the smallest one of the men said. "He's upstairs in bed now."

Aaron went up the stairs and met his mother coming down.

"Dad's got the flu, and I'm trying to break his fever right away," she said to him. Then in a whisper she added: "He's been out trying to do too much in all that weather." Then out loud again she said, "You go on and say hello, and hear what you can do, but please be careful you don't stay too long. And please don't you get it, too."

Aaron went on in, and already his parents' room seemed stuffy and laundry-like, the way rooms always seemed to get when someone was lying sick in them. His father looked strange, lying among all the soft blankets, in bed in broad daylight.

"Hello," his father said with a short grin, and a

kind of squeezed voice. "Ma says I've let—too many germs in. An' Rog's off to Min'ap'lis. But th' weather's clearin'. An' those fellas—'ve got jus' one more day. They jus' need some'n who knows this lake. Tomorra, early—you get your firs' chance a b'come a guide."

When Aaron came back downstairs, a boat's motor was whirring from out on the bay. It was two older people from another of the cabins, out for an evening ride. The three men, his mother said, had gone back to their cabin. Aaron walked on down to the dock, to where the two guide boats lay quietly waiting, like two traps. Each boat was eighteen feet long and had two motors bolted on at the stern: a big motor for getting quickly from place to place, and a smaller motor for steadying the boat while fishing. Aaron knew there wasn't a chance that either the boats or their motors were out of order.

He thought of ways of putting them out of order. He thought of ways of botching things up tomorrow so badly his father wouldn't ever send him out guiding again. Or ever let him go anywhere else, either.

He saw the water blankly reflecting the darkening sky, without a riffle, and he sniffed and felt of the crisp dry air, and he knew he couldn't hope for the weather to turn stormy again. Overhead, like long black-and-white arrows, three loons sped across the

sky in an absolutely straight line.

Suddenly, as always—wild and sharp and musical—a loon somewhere on the water began its evening calling. The flying loons kept flying straight over the weedy island that was a kind of northern "shore" for Rennin's Bay, on over the jagged tops of more distant pine trees they went, easily bound for wherever they wanted to be. *Me, too!* he thought. *I'll get off to the timber.*

Sure! he thought. *A good, full day's guiding. That ought to be enough. Then I'll say to him: See, I can do that, too, and I've helped you out. Now you ought to help me.*

Then he could tell if his father actually meant to ever let him go. If not, he'd go anyway—somehow. But it'd be easier and better not to have to sneak off.

Sure, Aaron promised himself. *This is a good chance. Nils is wrong.*

6

HE LAY STRETCHED *out once more at the edge of the familiar patch of straight stems and long, half-curled leaves. His pale stripes—pale with the color of the sunlit and part-sandy bottom—were still dark enough to hide him against the weeds, even in clear weather. His fins were quietly fanning in rhythm with the water's drifting. His wide jaws were closed tight. His eyes—*

He saw the school of yellow perch shifting in aimless patterns above him. He was not surprised. Sooner or later perch always came by this weed bed.

He knew how to wait until one fish near the edge of the school started a short movement away; then he would charge, and if the perch darted farther away he would overtake it, and if the perch took an extra moment to stop and turn, it would have to race past the muskie's jaws.

He hadn't planned his method. He had never even thought about it. It had simply happened once, and then again, and now it was all a habit. The habit had made him grow long and thick fast, fast enough to avoid the jaws of the perch, and of the other muskies and northern pike that also roamed his waters. Once they had all been bigger than he was.

It was his habit now also to lie here when the ache of hunger was in him, comfortably knowing the distances around him, comfortably waiting for the right moment, the right target: then with a racing charge he would end his hunger.

But now, though the thunder was gone and the surface was still, it was hard to wait. Already since the storm he had charged twice—too soon. And yet a restlessness still shook inside him, and his tensed muscles kept pressing to snap loose. He quivered, watching the perch, and simply went like a slipped arrow. Too soon. The perch exploded in a confusion of movement. He had no target, he had to pause, and the perch all scattered among the weeds that had hidden him, which now protected them.

He began to prowl around the weed bed, feeling his hunger more sharply and wanting to do the familiar thing, to wait, but something kept shaking him on. Unable to relax, unable to pause, the muskie kept circling, hunting what was bothering him, until the

34

restlessness itself began to feel familiar. He began moving away from the weed bed, this way and that, in graceful, purposeless dartings, but always returning, then going out again, trying to remember: where was he to go? why was he to go? 1481937

7

SUDDENLY FULL OF enthusiasm to learn more about guiding, Aaron ran back to the lodge, and quietly hurried up to see his father. His father was drowsy with medicine and wasn't able to stay awake long enough to answer many questions.

"Kee' doin' where you know— No tellin'—when or where a big muskie—migh' strike—" his father murmured. "Go 'head—have fun—"

His mother said the same things at breakfast. "Have fun," she said. "And Aaron, be careful! Maybe you'd better stay off the main lake."

In the first dawn light, the dock boards sounded loud and hollow under his feet. Rennin's Bay was smothered by a cool, damp mist; the water was obviously still smooth. Then little riffles swished about, and the boat bonked against the dock as he partially stepped, partially jumped down into it. It was Roger's boat.

Aaron got out his list. He checked the float gauges on the two red gas tanks to make sure they read *Full*, then opened the tanks to make sure the gauges were right. He checked the mixture dials on the motors to make sure they were set for the right combination of air and gas—though he might have to adjust them later. He made sure that the fuel line of the big motor was open and that of the little motor was shut, that both throttles were off and their propellers at neutral. He checked for the life jackets, the anchor, bailing bucket, the oars and oarlocks, the gaff and net and tackle box. For the stringer for hooking any caught fish to the boat, and the toolbox and matches and flashlight, and the slim post with the triangular red flag, which his father and brother had fashioned to set up as a triumphal banner whenever they'd caught a muskie—

"I thought your brother was going to guide us," said a voice over him.

He hadn't even heard their feet on the dock boards, but the three men were standing there above him. The smallest man stood in front, dressed now in tan khakies that were bulky around his thin body. He had a smooth, small, almost square face. His ears were thin and sharp, his lips were wide and thin, his eyes were glaring in their thin, wide slits.

37

"Isn't your brother going to guide us?" He wasn't simply repeating his question. He was demanding an answer.

Behind him the tall thin man was wearing khaki trousers and a long shooting jacket, which made him seem much taller. His face was steep and thin, and from the dock he seemed to stretch upward like a leafless winter tree. His eyes kept peering down from above his long thin nose like the eyes of a half-hidden and curious squirrel.

The other man—with thick round eyes and puffy cheeks above dark green clothing—said, "Do you know anything about this business, son?"

"Sure," said Aaron, gruffly; but it was difficult to make any kind of answer into their stares. "Rog's away. In Minneapolis," he added, because the short thin man kept glaring.

"I don't know—" said the man in green. He was a little tall, and a little bit fat, or soft, all over, and during the past week he had been kindly looking. Now he seemed to be suspecting something. "It's good to start young," he said. "But there's things a fella can't know or do without experience."

"It's just taking our money. That's all," hissed the short thin man. "I'm going to get it back, or get a guide."

"Just a minute," said the tall thin man, with his deep, sure voice, and his curious eyes high above.

"Young man, do you intend to drink whiskey while you're guiding us?"

"Huh?" said Aaron. "Me? Heck no."

The tall thin man nodded and seemed pleased. "Like father, like son," he said. "Do you intend to smoke a pipe?"

"No," said Aaron.

"One step better than your father," the man said. "Those clouds of pipe smoke your father kept sending up the past week made me think I was aboard a steamboat that was using damp peat moss for fuel. It's a wonder he didn't get sick sooner. But I suppose he's used to it. Now, tell me, do you know exactly where the muskies lie and guarantee that we will get one?"

"No," said Aaron, loudly and firmly.

"Gentlemen," said the tall thin man, "the lad doesn't drink or smoke on duty, and makes no false claims to knowledge. I think we might do much worse elsewhere." Then, carrying his rod and tackle box, the man stepped forward off the dock, reaching a long thin leg down into the boat as easily as if he were walking down stairs.

The other two hesitated and shrugged and sighed and paused, and then set down their gear and grasped the dock-edge, finally stretching, hesitatingly, down into the boat.

Aaron wanted to shout at them that he didn't want them to come, either—any of them. He didn't want to spend the rest of his life dragging people like them around the lake, every day, for what almost always would be no reason at all.

But he didn't shout. It was his father he had to talk to. A good day's guiding could do his talking for him. He got busy taking the men's equipment and placing it about the boat where he thought it'd be handy but out of the way. Then he energetically began priming the gas into the big motor by squeezing the bulb that bulged out of the hose from one gas tank. And he checked his gauges and controls again. He was unhappy, and scared even, but he could not afford to be thought stupid.

8

HE GRASPED THE handle of the starter cord and yanked.

The motor grumbled sleepily and quit.

He yanked again.

The motor sputtered and stopped.

Again.

More weak muttering. The sickly smell of gasoline began spreading through the air.

He had primed too much. The motor was flooded. There was nothing to do but wait until enough gas drained back out of the motor. Aaron had nothing to do then but sit and look at the three men looking back at him. He tried to look nonchalantly by them and up at the sky, which was turning into a solid misty pink as the dawn light began to brighten above the fog.

Finally, he chanced yanking the cord again. The motor started. For a few seconds he sat letting the rumbling and bubbling sounds grow more rhythmic. He tested the throttle, and the motor roared. He moved the throttle back, shifted from neutral to forward, and eased the throttle open again. The motor growled easily, and the boat started away from the dock, then swung back and banged the dock, then jerked toward open water as Aaron automatically fought with the steering-arm; but the boat swept in against the dock again, and Aaron quickly shut the motor. He'd forgotten to untie the snubbing lines.

Now as he untied the lines, he could scarcely care about the three staring faces, because the thought that his father and mother might be watching him from the lodge windows was burning a hot hole in the back of his neck.

Then, with the motor re-started, he remembered his father's voice many times saying, *"Accidents can happen, but anyone who drowns in this lake is a fool. And I'm not going to let any of my guests be fools."*

Looking full into the three faces, Aaron had to say, "I'm not supposed to leave the dock until everybody puts on his life jacket."

He had, then, to bend over and put on his own bright orange jacket; and even over the idling rumble of the motor, he could hear the short thin man snort, and the man in green sigh; and he heard the tall thin

man say, "Come now, Bert, the lad is only carrying out orders."

After that Aaron opened the throttle once more, and the boat slid forward onto Rennin's Bay. The mist was beginning to thin rapidly away. He eased the throttle steadily up to traveling speed. The sky was becoming a glowing candle-orange, and the orange was beginning to color the smooth, windless water. As it cut through the water, the boat made a constant tearing sound. Aaron felt like a droning fly scratching across the smooth orange eye of some giant resting animal, with the pines all around the edges like dark eyebrows. He felt that any moment a dark, hard paw was going to sweep from the sky and fling him off.

Instead, high and thin, beyond the tearing sounds and the motor roar, a loon screamed in false misery. And while searching for it, Aaron saw the familiar lodge and cabins and beach all drifting farther and farther behind him, attached to him now only by the motor's wake that was fast spreading and dying out in the calm water.

When he looked forward again, he saw that the boat was aiming rapidly toward Weed Island.

Weed Island was only a thin, overgrown reef jutting out from the shallow weed bed that grew along the western shore of the bay. Herons liked to stand along the island hunting frogs and small fish. By late summer a man could usually slog out to it from the west shore without getting his knees wet. In these high waters of springtime it was fun to dodge a boat past the island through those weeds and beat several minutes off the regular trip around the island to the first muskie area.

He'd done it with his dad several times. But now the motor was roaring directly behind him; his own hand was vibrating with the steering-arm, and Aaron was steering over the shoulders of three strange men. Weed Island loomed steadily closer. He lost his nerve. He started to swing the rudder the other way, to head for the clear, marked channel around the other end of the island. But the powerfully thrusting motor didn't want to change course. Aaron tugged hard and couldn't move the steering-arm. Then he lunged against it.

The boat veered as if in sharp anger, tilting steeply, and cold, wet spray suddenly came lashing in over the low side. Aaron yanked back, one foot quickly braced against the side to help him, and the boat rolled swiftly back, skidding steeply into a curve the other way. Aaron swung again against the steering-arm. He was remembering how much fight to expect. He got the boat leveled and aimed at the east end of the island, keeping it at full speed, the way his brother always did.

The men, having been swung from side to side,

were clutching at the gunwales with their hands; now they looked steadily also at the two fast-approaching narrow lines of posts, sticking hard and rigid out of the water, marking the dug channel out of Rennin's Bay. A tern was perched atop each post, each bird like a small gray lantern, until it began fluttering away.

They always fly when a boat gets close. They always do! Aaron thought.

But the terns deserting the posts sapped his confidence again. He gave up trying to roar between them. He twisted back the throttle and chewed down his pride. The motor subsided; the boat settled scratching and swishing deeper in the water, immediately slowing.

Slow and putter-putt, Aaron steered through the channel, curving gradually onto the long flat oval of Feather Bay. He could see the green man, seated heavily on the front thwart, softly shaking his head.

Right in front of Aaron the short thin man was glaring at him like a cornered cat.

From the middle of the boat, the tall thin man's voice, deep and sort of amused, almost chuckling, said, "Inexperienced, yes; reckless, no. There's room for hope, gentlemen. We could have done worse."

46

9

THE SHADOW OF *a boat passed quickly over him, and he rose after it.*

Like a huge long-nosed bullet, he broke through the bubbles spewing back from the motor. He kept following, hidden in the roiled water of the wake and poking curiously close to the furiously thrashing propeller. The metal blades could chop him up in an instant, and he sensed the danger. He had always sensed the danger, and then the sour, oily substance always spreading from it. He slowed back among the bubbles, then the thrashing suddenly began changing direction and he turned away into calmer, quieter water.

He saw the greenish cloudiness of other weeds ahead, and he drifted toward them.

His hunger wasn't bothering him so much. It was

his restlessness that ached inside him. Yet he still wanted to settle among weeds, to wait and watch, tensed but unmoving, as usual.

But he spied two thin streams of smaller bubbles and instantly was rushing toward them, scarcely disturbing the water, hearing the light swish-swish noises of the two ducks paddling ahead along the surface.

He was beneath the ducks before they saw or felt him coming. Their wings beat and they splattered wildly along the surface with his jaws cruising just beneath them. He never opened his mouth; the ducks lifted frantically into the air, and the muskie kept cruising.

He had remembered other bubbles. His restlessness was more exciting. He swam in long, sweeping arcs, anxious to find the right direction.

10

AARON AGAIN HAD the motor roaring and the boat rushing through the calm orange-glowing water, carrying them along the northern shore of Weed Island, toward the cove where the route through the weedy shallows would have brought them. There the bottom of Feather Bay went down like a dragon's throat, a hundred and eight feet deep at the center.

"You can catch walleye perch from the middle of that hole," his father once had told him, *"if you'd ever want to bother."*

Aaron aimed into the cove and shut the big motor off completely. The boat again quickly settled scratching and swishing into the flat water.

"You can cast at the edges of this cove," he said aloud. "There's usually about six feet of water now, and muskie weeds."

Then he carefully and nervously primed and pulled the small motor. When it started, he began to steer the boat in a slow circle about the edge of the cove.

"What kind of bait plug does our *guide* suggest?" the short thin man said tightly.

"Anything orange works good," Aaron said.

"*Tell 'em anything handy,*" Roger had once said. "*Who knows what makes a fish bite?*"

"Why didn't you tell me that in time, *Mr. Guide?*" said the short thin man. "I left my orange socks and tie in the cabin."

The soft man in green laughed moistly.

The tall thin man stood slowly up in the center of the boat. From the tip of his fishing rod dangled a bright red piece of metal, with a tuft of black deer's hair hanging from it concealing the claw of three barbed hooks. He lifted the rod back and started to flick it forward when, even before the bait could fly, the whole sky burst into gleaming yellow, and black shadows fell among the yellow-glowing weeds and trees along the shore. Then the tall man's bait was soaring, and the rim of the sun, showing above the water and forests behind them, made its small splash glitter.

Another loon cried. A cold, light breeze began flowing out of the West. With the breeze came the sound of a motor, not sharp and droning as a boat's motor would have sounded, but a low, drumming roar, muffled by the half-mile thickness of pine woods standing between Feather Bay and the highway: the day's first logging truck was heading for the sawmill in town, over on the shore of Feast Lake. Aaron wondered if Nils were riding in it.

The gleaming yellow sunlight grew brighter, but paler; the shadows seemed to become less severe. Aaron sat and kept the small, chuggling motor pushing the boat slowly around the cove. A heron passed over on slowly moving wings; the twittering of small birds had begun along the shore. After a while another low drumming sound went along the hidden highway. From the other direction a boat's motor began to drone, and then it faded away. It was Saturday morning, but the season was early and cool. There probably would not be too many other boats.

"Look!" said Aaron.

The three men, midway in the motions of casting out or reeling in, looked at him and then toward the spot where he was pointing: at a blob moving through the light waves that the breeze had started.

"Turtle," Aaron said. "A snapper."

"They get pretty big, don't they?" the short thin man said, saying it toward the other two men.

"You bet," said Aaron.

"And snappers make the best eating," said the

softer, fatter man, looking out at the movement in the water.

"Some people make a living just catching them and selling them for food in Minneapolis," Aaron said, though he'd only just heard that and didn't know if it was true or not.

"When they get twice as big and learn to leap, I'll fish for them," said the tall thin man, and he cast his line toward the shore again.

"But they make good soup," said the soft man in green.

"At least we'd get *something*," said the short thin man. "We've been here a week with nothing."

"Just how do you propose to reach that turtle?" asked the tall thin man, steadily reeling in his bait with short jerks to give it lifelike movements.

"Will they strike a plug?" the short thin man said suddenly at Aaron.

Aaron didn't know. "Sometimes, maybe," he said.

The short thin man twisted around and flung his orange wooden plug with its three clusters of hooks toward the moving shape. The bait splashed close by it, and the shape disappeared.

"So much for turtles, gentlemen," said the tall thin man, lifting his bucktail back out of the water, and then casting again toward the shore.

But behind him the turtle surfaced again.

"There— If we got close we could scoop it up with

a net," said the short thin man.

"It'll probably just dive and stay down if we move close," moaned the soft green man.

"It will," said the tall thin man.

"I know how!" said Aaron. "Pull in your lines!" he said—commanded. The force of his voice surprised himself and the others.

The tall thin man stared and hesitated, but obeyed. "A guide must guide, I suppose," he sighed.

If the others said anything more, Aaron didn't hear them. He was loosening the net, and he was intent on the turtle now; his feelings were buzzing with the chance to do something and catch something.

The turtle was swimming steadily toward the weedy shallows that separated the cove from Rennin's Bay on the other side, the shallows he had avoided by going around the other end of Weed Island.

"Get this ready up front," Aaron said.

With a smile cheering his soft face, the man in green quickly put away his rod and took up the net as it was handed forward to him. He knelt on the bow thwart, leaning forward, anxious.

Aaron started the big motor and quickly throttled it down and left it idling in neutral. Then he aimed the boat at the swimming turtle and let the small motor putter them forward as near as he dared, without alarming the turtle. The turtle was close to going out of reach into the weeds. Aaron turned off the small motor.

"Be ready," he said. "We'll swing past him fast, before he can dive. One—two—*three!*"

In one motion Aaron put the big motor in Forward and spun the throttle. The big motor roared, and the boat shot forward, right out from under him almost— except that the motor struck him in the back and kept him aboard amid a smothering rush and a blurred swaying full of wind and roar; then he felt a sudden slowing, and a high whining noise. A sputter-

ing. Then stillness.

The sky reappeared directly above him; the boat was all around him. The short thin man was lying beside him, as if asleep, with his head propped against the thwart he had been sitting on.

Getting up on his knees, Aaron saw the tall thin man sitting strangely high above the edge of the boat with the net circling down over his long, thin face like a beekeeper's helmet. Underneath him was the soft man in green.

Over the gunwales Aaron could see the weeds of

the shallows all around him, and he knew before he looked that weeds were wrapped snug as ropes around the propellers of both motors, especially the biggest, holding the boat tight.

He looked a moment for the turtle, too, but saw only the weeds and the water.

11

HE HAD FOUND *a straight direction. He was still uncertain but it felt right, and he swam it steadily, while the lake bottom dipped into darkness, then rose near him with the pale-bright tans and greens of sand and thin weeds. He slowed here, without actually stopping. He liked the half-shady, shallow warmth—yet not completely.*

He searched about puzzled, discontented, but not for food.

Then close to the surface, in the warming sun of the warming season, he swam on, following his direction—but veering off at the slightest hint of shallow shade, or to follow the touches of warmer water currents—gradually returning to his direction.

12

HE HAD TO just sit and watch.

The tall thin man kept reaching way over the motors, head downward, his arms jerking deep in the cold springtime water.

"Whyn't you let the boy cut at those weeds? He's our guide, isn't he?" The short thin man kept slowly, steadily rubbing around the aching spot on his head.

"Because he might fall in and get chilled," the tall thin man grunted. "Then we'd have to go back to the lodge. We'd be done fishing. Done for a whole year."

"We'll be done tonight, anyway," the soft green man wailed from the bow. "This is our last day, and look how we're spending it."

It's not my fault, Aaron told himself. *I was trying to get them a turtle. I'd try to get these weeds loose, too.* But the tall thin man had insisted, and it seemed that to argue would only make what they'd tell his father worse.

Aaron had to just sit and listen. He heard several logging trucks pass along the highway; one was empty, jingling with slack chains as it headed back to the timberlands. He felt the air above the water growing warmer, the mosquitoes rising; time passing.

Finally the tall thin man straightened up; the skin on his long thin arms was red and dripping with the cold water. "I've freed us, gentlemen," he announced. And Aaron quickly grabbed an oar and poled the boat back out into open water. He started just the small motor because he wasn't going far. The men couldn't fish while traveling, and he needed the men to catch a muskie. A muskie on his first day of guiding ought to be all his father should expect from anyone.

So he steered the boat just out of the cove and across the mouth of a broad but twisting channel that led inward from another bay—Bay Michele. Again the men began casting as he puttered slowly along the weedy shore. Already Aaron was thinking *If not here, where? Where next?* For Feast Lake was really a flowage: a whole chain of lakes, or bays, reaching across fifteen or twenty miles of country, and who knew where a hungry and foolish fish might be? On the maps Feast Lake looked like a big blue pear, with the bays and channels that Aaron knew lying like a blue, leafy twig to the Southwest. Other bays branched out from the other sides of Feast Lake. Water from a thousand short little streams emptied into the bays and channels and moved gradually into the main lake and from there out into the Feast River and on southward toward the Mississippi. But anyone could know that. It was northward in the wide, incompletely mapped forests spreading through Turtle County and on into Canada that there were new things sure to be found, and stout timber sure to be cut and brought out just for getting at it and doing it.

After he'd watched the three men spend another half-hour of useless casting out and reeling in, Aaron gathered up his voice and spoke out that they ought to move.

By bringing in their baits and silently sitting down, the men agreed. Then through his wide thin lips the short thin man said, "Now let's move fast and straight. Our time's a-wasting."

Quickly Aaron got the big motor roaring and headed them toward the other end of Feather Bay. As soon as they left the sheltered western shoreline, they began splashing along with the waves being pushed up by the breeze that had begun at sunrise.

Aaron knew they were swiftly getting close to The Pasture, a weedy shallows that didn't come quite to the surface. He knew it was better muskie ground than most, and he began searching the shore

lines. But he wasn't sure he could line up quickly between the right landmarks. He knew his father, or
even Roger, could find it fast, and he didn't want
these men going back and mentioning that he
couldn't. He didn't want them staring at him while
he searched for another weed-shallows. He didn't
want to risk the time. He kept the big motor roaring
and didn't shut it off till he'd swung around the north
point of Swimmers' Island and into the windbreak of
its thick pines.

Immediately the men were up and fishing. Quickly
Aaron started the small motor and kept the boat
sliding slowly ahead on the flat sunny water, until
after about the length of three football fields he
forced the boat to turn and start bumping and splashing back to windward around the cliff at the south
end of the island.

Three times around Swimmers' Island they went,
with the sun getting steadily higher and the wind
steadily warmer. Aaron sat like another wooden part
of the boat while the men sat balancing and casting
through the rough water, and stood up for the
smooth. They never stopped hurriedly casting out
and reeling in, busily making their baits soar and
splash and wriggle back, waving their short rods like
mad magicians trying to produce from the darkly
boiling or bright and silky water a magic appearance:
a miracle that wouldn't come.

13

RESTLESS, TOO; *in pure rage at being invaded, a young muskie struck up out of new weeds. The weeds were in dark mud bottom so the young muskie had darker stripes than the older, but it had the same needle teeth and rubbery power. The older muskie heaved out of his straight gliding, diving to get away. He wasn't used to being attacked, but dove quick enough to feel only a stinging scratch along his tail— Then he slashed upward.*

The young muskie saw his mistake and tried to escape, but had to fight. From barely a length away they rushed, struck: accidentally caught each other's jaws, and twisted over and over each other, braiding themselves through the water with whiplash strokes, though the huge and heavy water showed scarcely a ripple. Down they went, into the weeds, and churned up dark mud from the bottom, until the young mus-

kie, too short and slender to keep up the struggle, broke and fled darting into the curtaining weeds, racing from his hunting ground.

The bigger muskie forgot him and flickered on into the vastness of water.

14

THEY HAD LEFT the big island.

They had circled, and circled, and circled the small island beyond—a hump so thickly covered with the remains of burnt trees it looked like the back of a sunken porcupine.

Through the rough water of the windward side or the smoothness of the sheltered side the men kept casting out and reeling in, sitting down or standing up, while Aaron sat constantly regulating the throttle, steering round and round, till he felt with a sudden sickening in his stomach that he was handling the boat too well—that unless they brought in a muskie today his father would simply get in the habit of sending him out, again and again, until it would be too late. Like Nils'd said, he'd start spending nearly all the rest of his life this way: guiding emptily round and round, in the very same places.

Some other boats had begun arriving near them, and Aaron watched in dread of seeing someone catch a fish where he had just been.

But the other boats seemed only to keep proving there was nothing there to be caught.

"Please, Mr. Guide, don't you know *any* place where there's fish?" the soft man up front cried out.

"We are simply following the same route and method that his father did for five days, gentlemen," said the tall thin man. "There is no imagination in this. Only a blind hope in luck."

"We'll move," said Aaron.

The men reeled in, and he changed to the big motor; the boat sped into the wind and waves, back across the long, finger-like stretch of Feather Bay, and into the twisting channel to Bay Michele. Lost in the motor's roar, Aaron pretended that he was bringing a logging truck out of a thick, wild forest that he was opening up with his own saws and steady work; it was another full load. He pretended that he already knew how to stack the logs so they wouldn't slip, and that he knew how to drive the trucks.

He steered the boat under the bridge that carried the road from Turtle County. No real logging trucks were passing.

In the middle of crossing Bay Michele, he saw a snake. It was a garden snake—just a thin flash of wrig-

gling color was all, but for an instant it was plain.
Automatically Aaron heaved the boat after it. Again
the men had to grasp to hang on; again water splashed
in over the gunwales. And a bright blue speedboat
Aaron hadn't seen—till that moment—that had been
racing along behind him, was suddenly very large and
charging at them.

Aaron flung himself back at the steering-arm, trying to turn the guide boat back straight and away
from the speedboat. He saw the speedboat growing
taller above flashing white spray, then lost sight of it
as the guide boat rolled and skidded as it changed its

curve, then he saw it again, much bigger. He kept twisting the throttle as hard as he could. The speedboat started to keel over; Aaron hunched up and felt crushed and deafened by a double roar and a thump ing of water; a shadow flickered, and he kept clinging in the swift, tilted new curve of the guide boat as he was suddenly also being heaved up and down as the wake from the speedboat tumbled up over his own. Then the guide boat had swung full around and was bucking head-on into the wakes, and Aaron saw the blue speedboat churning away in its own escaping curve. He fought with the steering-arm and throttle and got his brother's boat down into slow, even movement.

"We were almost killed! We were almost killed!" screamed the soft green man up front.

The short thin man right in front of Aaron sharply snarled, "Boy guides! Swindlers!"

"It was a snake. I saw a snake," Aaron cried out loudly. "A small snake. I wanted to see if it was in trouble way out here from shore."

"Please, please, let's stay with *fish*," pleaded the soft green man.

"It was all for knowledge and kindness, gentlemen. All for knowledge and kindness," said the tall thin man, in his same deep voice; but the friendly tone he'd used at the dock had completely gone.

The snake had vanished also; who could tell which

way, among nothing but wind-chopped water. Aaron couldn't find the courage right then to suggest they look. So he had to go on. He turned up the throttle and once more escaped the men's voices as he steered the boat across the bay, past a moored seaplane, and into a longer, shady, and weed-narrowed channel that led to Mink Bay; he wondered whether the snake had been safe or not, and whether he might have helped it, and could see no hope of ever knowing.

Meanwhile he was still following his father's method, which was to try first in the first places, then go far away fast and work slowly back, to be ever closer to home in case the weather should begin to change. The real farthest places would be out across the main lake, but he didn't want to have to go out there. He would stay in the bays. But he'd follow his father's method so his father wouldn't be able to say he was foolish.

Besides, he was going to Mink Bay because it was small and well-protected against the west wind. It might be the best fishing water today. It would feel good to have the woods close about him.

He found the protection complete. The tops of the thick pines on the shores were all swaying some, but the short spread of water was calm and flat. The still air about the bay had grown hot under the sun. Drops of sweat began to glisten on the men's faces as they went on with more casting out and reeling in, the tall thin man always jerking his bait as he reeled. Mosquitoes began drifting around them in the close-to-shore stillness. They kept Aaron pestered, though the men weren't bothered as much because they could keep moving. They moved in dead silence now. In the timber there was always shouting and laughing, and—he'd never realized it till now—a great freedom to stretch and move about.

The short thin man suddenly stopped and took off his life jacket and then his khaki jacket. His tan shirt underneath was dark with patches of sweat. The man began to fish again.

Aaron's head buzzed with what he ought to do.

Then the tall thin man untied his life jacket and unsnapped his shooting-style jacket and let the two slide off together, hardly missing a cast.

Aaron breathed in and said, "I'm sorry but I'm not supposed to carry anyone without a life jacket on."

The short thin man sniffed and scowled and made another cast.

The tall thin man said, "I don't believe you'll have to carry me, young man."

Aaron got angry. The rule was for their own good, just like the helmets in the woods, where he'd never heard anyone arguing about them. But he still wasn't used to ordering grown men around.

"If you don't put on your life jackets, I'm supposed to start home," he said, but it came out lightly.

"Oh, just hush and keep that motor perking," said the short thin man. "Who's paying for this outing?"

"There is insolence in all young people these days, gentlemen," said the tall thin man. "It's best just to ignore it."

Aaron punched at the small motor's button and stopped it. "We're going in," he stated loudly, hoping the pounding nervousness inside him didn't show. He didn't care whether they went in now or not. He'd tried with the turtle. He'd been trying to find fish. He'd been trying to do something good when they'd almost crashed with the speedboat, which had been racing too close behind anyway. Though that wasn't how it was going to sound when he got home. But he'd be better off going home now, still a guide doing his work; if he gave in to them he'd be just a kid who drove the motor, with nothing to convince his father to let him go up to the timber.

"Put that motor back on," the short thin man hissed.

"Young man, you're being insolent and doing your family no good," said the tall thin man.

"If you don't put on your jackets, I'm going in," Aaron insisted tensely.

"Get that motor back on," snapped the short thin man, laying down his rod, "or I'll whip you over my knee."

"Please, please, let's stick to fishing," the soft green

70

man called out.

"No fishing without life jackets!" exclaimed Aaron.

"I think you'd better come sit up front awhile," said the tall thin man; he was reeling his bait directly in, not bothering with his little action tugs. The short thin man was already shifting across his thwart toward him, and Aaron saw he had only a second to get started or he'd lose to them. He yanked at the big motor. It was unflooded and barked instantly to life.

All at once, the three men sat down and grabbed at the gunwales. Aaron had hold of the big motor's throttle and gear lever.

"Wait!" shouted the tall thin man.

"Please, please, let's stick to fishing," wailed the soft green man.

"Leave that motor alone!" the short thin man ordered.

Tensely Aaron kept holding the controls, watching the tense looks in the men's faces, through several moments.

"Never—" the short thin man finally said, "Never have I been so robbed and cheated and shoved about." Then, slowly, he began slipping his life jacket on over just his shirt.

The tall thin man, with a face of ice, started slipping his life jacket back on.

Then the soft man in green, still wearing his life jacket, stood back up and began fishing.

When his orange strings were tied fast, the short thin man stooped and picked up his rod. With a jolt Aaron saw the man suddenly, quickly and faintly, smile at him.

Aaron turned the big motor back off, but he kept one hand on its starter.

15

HE SWAM HIS *straight line through the bright green glimmering of wet daylight. Beneath him the water was blue, gray, black. He could feel the cool hollowness of very deep bottom. He swam until weeds and dark ground rose out of those depths, then he swam excitedly on into a long, warm reach of still water, crowded with weeds in places and filled with old stumps and tangled, sunken limbs. He drifted on among this stiff wood and softer, flooded weeds until the water grew very shallow, and he felt a tingling, an almost shivering alertness.*

Here and there little groups of bubbles were rising where crawdads and other small creatures on the bottom had moved. Other tiny puffs fluttered upwards here and there as gases escaped from bits of rotting wood. In one place a small noisy cloud of bubbles was constantly dancing as a flooded stream kept emptying into the quiet marsh.

In this cove six years ago he had hatched from his egg, swimming around with part of his egg sac puffed beneath his jaw. When he had no more food in it, he had caught his first insects and then minnows here, and from the shadows he had darted after the bubbles, scarcely able to let the clusters move without investigating every one of them. The exercise had helped make him strong and quick.

The habit, too, had lingered.

Again he began to tease at the bubbles, settling on the bottom then floating up after them.

But the water was too shallow, and the muskie was too big and quick now for the bubbles to keep him interested. He wanted to rush, and turn, and travel—except he could no longer feel a direction. The warmth felt just right. He began to fin rapidly. But he stayed still, in the dense shade of a stump.

His own color began to darken.

16

THE FISH STRUCK just as they returned to Bay Michele; Aaron saw water crash up around the tall thin man's first cast. He heard the man gasp. He saw the bent rod suddenly lifted high and shivering at the tip. Then the fish was running, for the reel at the man's hand buzzed as its handle spun like a small propeller, with only the man's thumbs against the reel, keeping the line snug but letting it unwind so it wouldn't get broken.

Aaron was up on one knee; his breath was stopped, but his heart was pounding; he kept working with the small motor, keeping the boat broadside to the run. The other two men were frantically reeling in their own lines to get them out of the way.

The fish sounded—went down. The line stopped flickering; it stretched stiffly.

Then with a wild grunt the tall thin man grasped at his reel, trying to wind in, fumbling in his hurry. His line began to lay loosely forward in the water.

Aaron snapped at his controls and made the boat start backwards.

"Not so fast! Not so fast! You'll snap my line!" bellowed the tall thin man.

He'll toss the hook if you don't tighten faster, thought Aaron.

The fish again broke the surface; it kept spraying water here and there, and the tightened line kept sweeping after it. Aaron put the motor in neutral.

The rushing stopped, but the line stayed taut, and the tall thin man was reeling again, one thin hand tensely jerking round and round; with each twist he had to decide whether to reel more and risk a sudden fight that would snap the line, or to pause to wait for a hint and risk having the bait thrown.

Aaron shut off the motor to stop the knife-edged propeller. But his heart had stopped pounding, too. He began to squirm and ache. There was still no leap—there'd been something in the rushing about—Suddenly a shape moved up beside the boat; its dark green top was at the surface, and its long speckled side gleamed just below. And the bucktail bait was bright at the corner of its long jaws. Feeling all stiff and hollow Aaron moved forward with the net.

"No, let me!" screamed the tall thin man. "You

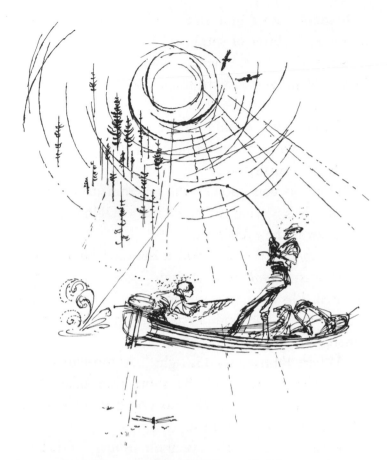

keep away! I've caught it!" The tall thin man kept a
grip on his rod with one hand and, with the other arm,
reached at the net. Aaron let him take it. Aaron
watched him sweep it into the water, but too quickly,
and from behind the fish. Yet the fish came up, heavy
and shining, balanced on the rim of the net, its long
jaws drooping.

It shook into a blur and splashed sharply, leaving an instant's glitter of spray still falling.

Then there was silence, and the red-and-black bucktail bait tangled with the net, alone in the water: water they could see into a little bit, but couldn't chase into. They could only sit.

"It was just a northern pike anyway," Aaron said finally, in a small voice.

"How do you know?" the tall thin man snapped out; he was staring at the water. "Didn't you see those jaws!" he exclaimed.

"It was a northern," nodded the short thin man.

"It was a *good* one, though!" the tall thin man shouted. His long face swung around like a hawk's. "That net! The kid keeps the net back there where—"

"Where I'd have used it right!" Aaron flared.

"It wasn't the net," the short thin man spoke sharply. "It was a chance, and you guessed wrong." He glared at the taller man.

"Please, please, let's stay with fishing," cried the soft green man up front. "*See:* the water's flat here, too. And the air's hotter. That's why the fish hit. The fishing time's coming on."

Then Aaron noticed, too, that the wind had died away. The reflection of the seaplane in the water was a clear picture. Bay Michele had become as flat as Mink Bay.

"Just feel that heat!" the soft green man said. "I betcha I'm going to eat muskie tonight."

"It'll be the one *I've* caught," grinned the short thin man. Then he bent over and swept up his rod. "Tally-ho!" he cried out to his bait as he cast it.

"Go get 'em, Flashy Hooks!" The soft green man cheered his bait from the bow.

Aaron yanked the small motor into life as if now everything was certain and it was only a matter of time before a muskie would be in the boat.

But the tall thin man seemed to move stiffly and darkly, like the swaying of a dead tree, as they went on, slowly fishing up one side of Bay Michele and down the other, motor-muttering along every weed bar and into every cove. Aaron kept sitting and searching the water ahead for his course. Plainly the men's arms were tired; their backs began slouching; but they wouldn't stop for lunch. This was their last day, and they *each* wanted a muskie.

The time went past one o'clock. There was no shade or breeze on the water, and the heat kept glaring down. Aaron grew more and more damp and itchy beneath his own life jacket.

"At my friend's timber camp we'd already have twenty bolts of lumber to show for all this work," he said.

"At home I'd have had a game of golf and the lawn mowed," said the short thin man.

"I'd eat sawdust for a week, for a muskie strike now," sighed the soft green man up front.

No one said anything more. They hadn't really even been talking to each other. Aaron felt he might as well have been sitting there all alone.

He noticed the short thin man right in front of him suddenly shift his balance and move very slowly, reeling like a cat softly pawing toward a bird. Aaron looked where the man was staring, and he saw the torpedo—rigid, brown, steadily coming just below the water, just behind the man's orange bait. He saw it seem to lengthen and darken as it came closer, with bright unblinking eyes staring, too.

The short thin man stopped reeling. The muskie bumped the bait. The bait floated limply at the surface. The muskie hung below the thin dangling hooks. Then it drifted still closer, like a dark shadow in the curtainy green of the sunlit water, and its thick strength showed clear as it rolled and sank a little, just out of reach. Its fins scarcely swished as it sank away, into deeper darkness.

It had been longer than a man's leg. And bigger.

Aaron didn't know what he might have done better, but it was maddening to have been so helpless. He looked at the short thin man and saw him looking up at the sky, but with his eyes closed and his mouth moving silently. Then the short thin man opened his eyes, looked around and saw Aaron watching him.

"Tell me about your friend's timber camp," the short thin man said sharply, swiftly. "Do they get much money for a bolt of lumber?"

"They—they—" Aaron stammered in surprise— "They get almost eighty dollars a load."

"How many loads a day?"

"One, for two people," Aaron answered energetically. "It depends on the kind of wood. And the kind of ground it's growing on."

The short thin man puckered his lips and nodded his head. He kept his thin brows wrinkled thoughtfully, and Aaron began tingling with eagerness, expecting him to ask another question any moment. But the short thin man just fished, and the other two men kept fishing, too, without ever having seen the muskie. The short thin man didn't mention it. Aaron never mentioned it either. It was a secret; and it felt better to have that than nothing.

17

HE KEPT STAYING, *quivering and nervous, in the cove where he had hatched and survived, unguarded and alone, six years before. The little silent puffs of bubbles here and there, and the bubbles in the noisily shaking cloud, kept moving upward as they always had. Suddenly there was a new shape in the dark, tangled shapes of old limbs. It moved, and the muskie flickered and stretched out in pursuit. The movement sped faster ahead of him, twisting, long and glittering, among the sunken wood, swirling thickly back from the edge of open water and rushing, swirling and flashing, at the surface among the grasses, and avoiding him.*

The muskie kept chasing, though the form he chased was much bigger than he was; it had always been this way. He could swirl no quicker. But he rushed a little swifter through the short straight open-ings, till, as the other muskie curved again, he tensed and shot low among the flooded clumps and swept up beside her.

She didn't offer to fight, or even pause, but darted and swirled and sped in ever-increasing curves among the stumps and limbs; and he swam beside, the two of them never missing a bend, or a signal, each of them slowing down, each the shadow of the other, smooth as cloud shadows. Finally she began spreading her eggs—a hundred, then a thousand she scattered in the calm water of the cove—ten thousand, fifty thousand, a hundred and fifty thousand eggs she let drift down to stick on the limbs or grasses—and he covered them with his milt to make them fertile. They left them unwatched and unprotected; he didn't even notice the first insects and minnows beginning to move to-ward the places he had been, feeding as busily as their nervousness let them.

They stayed swimming slowly together. For the first time he began to feel the faint smarting of the scratch along his tail. He began to feel crowded be-side this other muskie. He had no more patience with her, but neither was he tied. He drifted away from her promptly, but slowly and easily, and coasted among the dark shapes that were drab and dead, then silently swam back into clear water that was dark and cool with depth. He was still dark, too, and as he

83

traveled he kept flicking his tail but was unable to shake loose the thin cut, which kept smarting.

18

HE TRIED TO STOP when they came back out the twisting channel from Bay Michele and then again at the turtle's cove. But the sun was sliding westward. They went past Weed Island, quickly past the straight dug channel to Rennin's Bay, curving and rocking onward around other fishing boats still working near Swimmers' Island.

The orange life jackets were glaring; he'd been awake on the water ever since dawn, and when he closed his eyes, he had to force them open again. In the woods there was always shade, and the bright colored helmets moved around like cheery decorations.

The big motor kept roaring behind him, and the new wind, a warm south wind, kept dipping across Feather Bay at an angle, splashing low wave crests against them broadside. The speeding boat swayed like a hammock, yet kept getting closer to the small island that looked like a sunken porcupine. Aaron wanted to stop there, too, in the safer water. What difference would it make where they stopped, when they couldn't see what they were doing anyway?

But all that area had been fished, and the chances for a muskie were dimming; he'd have to be able to say to his father: "*At least I tried. I tried as far as I could go.*"

So he felt he had to try out on Feast Lake, too, or the little spirits that always watched things wouldn't let him get to go to the timber.

Ahead the wooded shores of Feather Bay gradually shouldered toward each other, but stopped before they sealed the bay from the water beyond. Deer were sometimes seen wading across on the shallow rock ledge that marked the boundary between the Bay and the Lake, and if the boat were swayed there he might bang the propeller. The shear-pin would snap, letting the motor run without jamming and breaking more parts before he could turn it off. Then the motor would have to be tilted up, and the shear-pin —and possibly a bent or cracked prop—replaced. An awkward job, especially in wavy water, and it would take time; Aaron felt that even the spirits wouldn't mind if he slowed down a little now.

The big motor seemed to grow smaller as well as

slower and quieter, for beyond the ledge he could see Feast Lake starting to open out. He steered at the Deer Walk with his eyes uplifted, watching the highline electric wires that came looping over the narrows. A bright placard was swinging from them as a warning to low-flying airplanes, and Aaron remembered also that beneath it was a low, level place in the rock. He tried to steer so that the placard stayed directly in front of him; and with a moment's relief he watched it come directly over and pass beyond him.

Then he also saw, edging the long slit of northwestern sky which Feather Bay now held open behind him, the soapy smear of storm clouds.

He watched the low, slowly changing shapes for several moments, measuring their size and location. When he looked forward again, he was thoroughly onto Feast Lake. It was spreading away flat but rippling to its eastern shore, so distant that the woods there appeared gray instead of green and seemed to stand not half as tall as toothbrush bristles. To the North the water spread endlessly into the sky, its shore ten miles out of sight, inside Turtle County. The men so close in front of him seemed to be sitting almost in his lap. Once more they were staring at him.

Aaron started to tell them it didn't matter, that even *he* had enough experience to know those clouds were building too far to the north to bother Feast Lake.

Before he could speak the soft green man up front called unhappily at him, "Aren't we ever going to stop traveling and start fishing again?"

"Time's a-wastin', my friend," said the short thin man right in front of him.

Aaron shut off the big motor. He pointed at the near edge swinging away southeastward. "There's fish weeds all along there to town," he said abruptly.

Aaron started the small motor and sat back down, but he couldn't stay calm. He couldn't be sure about the storm clouds. He couldn't forget that to one side of him there was nothing but air and water, without a single stick poking up to mark the shallows and deeps, not the smallest island to break the sun's glare, or the sudden shifts of the wind. Even with his father he'd always gotten uneasy on Feast Lake.

He kept the boat following close along the southern shore, and he kept listening to the south breeze pushing through the treetops and watched the rows of waves each getting just a little bit taller with every roll. He kept thinking that if he lost his power, or had to cut it off to pull in a fish, the boat would start drifting immediately out into that vast, uncontrollable emptiness.

He felt himself listening too tensely to the sounds of the small motor, holding his breath waiting for the

88

slightest stutter. He kept turning also and looking back across the distance of water that was getting steadily longer between him and the Deer Walk, and up at the storm clouds now becoming visible above Feast Lake's western shore, like gray gorilla heads peering over jungle brush. He thought about the men who used to ride rafts and herds of floating logs across the whole exposed length of Feast Lake before they had big enough trucks. He'd be that brave, too, if he had the chance. He was sure he would. He just didn't want to risk everything too soon, for a fish that probably wouldn't even bite.

From the waves and tree sounds he began getting sure signs that the warm wind was strengthening. He spied, red and tan along the shore ahead, the docks of the Birch Shores Fishing Lodge.

He decided that when he'd gotten that far it would be enough; he'd use the storm clouds as an excuse to turn back.

19

HE SWAM CALM *and relaxed. He glided. He had time to notice the returning twinges of hunger. Light twinges now. Just enough to keep him alert and curious, and to help him forget again the mild hurt of his tail.*

He sensed the choppy movements of the water surface and began moving opposite to them, dimly knowing that this way he would reach many small fish in some calm, shallow water.

But the bottom began to rise abruptly, a gray steeply sloping wall of tumbled rocks and stones that steadily grew brighter and paler as he lifted beside it. He'd never come to shore at this place before. He became more alert. He began hearing whinings and rattlings—

He shot ahead and downward, away from a swiftly

growing shadow that blackened out the light. The water was struck a heavy blow; the concussion of it squeezed him as dark forms charged beneath the surface. He whirled in among some stones to guard his sides; now he lay tensed, his eyes and long jaws pointing back toward the attack.

But the shapes had gone back to the surface and were lying partly in and partly out of the water, rolling and jostling slowly sideways and forwards.

More shadows blackened over the surface. Another concussion immediately fell upon him, squeezing him. More huge, long forms burst down toward him, but went back up to join the others.

The muskie lay still, defensive, glaring, not comprehending—waiting, but finding nothing further to fear. Curiosity shivered him loose, and he began to rise again.

As he lifted, the whining and rattling sounds came back. And a smell. He had tasted the smell vaguely before; he had tasted older, staler samples of it often. The smell was heavy but there was no food in it. He saw small fish scurrying away as he approached, but the big, stiff, strangely moving shapes attracted him more.

He rose all the way to the surface, among the logs, and saw cloudlike smoke gushing low overhead from a dark hump beyond the water's edge. He swam about, finding no meanings anywhere and was about *to leave when there was a large, weedlike movement atop one of the logs. The movement had eyes—live eyes.*

The pond man, with spiked boots and sharp, hooked spear, came jumping and balancing, riding and guiding the floating logs toward the sawmill ramp as they were needed. The pond man stopped, just before making a stride. *The muskie, staring upward, felt the sudden aim of the eyes above him. Parts of that live shape swung upward and came quickly down. The muskie shook himself, lunging onward as something thin and quick slashed into the water.*

20

"bwaah!" said the tall thin man.

"What is it?" the other two exclaimed.

Aaron saw the man's rod had jerked straight upward again. But the deep voice was drab sounding: "A whole school of perch struck at my line. Some of them weren't as big as the bait."

"Perch! A good sign. There must be muskies close." The soft green man almost sang.

"If they're close, they won't be hungry," the short thin man muttered. "Many fish, bad fishing, some say."

Aaron felt himself holding back a hollow, unpleasant laugh, their talk was so foolish. And he was feeling calmer; he was getting a little more used to working on Feast Lake, and he was close to the Birch Shores docks.

He suddenly heard a reel rattling tightly. He quickly called for the others to reel in as he balanced alertly by the motor. The rattling stopped just as quickly, and he saw the soft green man's line straining rigidly among the offshore waves. *Walleye*, Aaron thought in disgust. Then he saw the man's plug bob up to the surface, covered only with weeds.

The soft green man hurried to untangle. Aaron immediately steered further from shore, for slightly deeper water. At least it had been a moment's excitement, though there was nothing to show but weeds; and there was nothing to do now but keep rocking over wave after wave, trying to stay close enough to the weed beds to attract a muskie, far enough out to avoid more fouling of weeds and bait. He was tired.

He revved the small motor another twist faster, to have more control. The wind was picking up, and the wind coursing through the treetops on shore seemed to get louder. It had grown so thick with dampness he could hardly breathe it. It kept flooding over him toward the huge gray and blue loaves of clouds, and white anvils of clouds, that had grown out of the gorilla heads he had seen earlier. Those clouds were constantly folding and reshaping, and slowly moving into the shoreless space above the northern rim of the lake.

"They can go eight or ten miles into the sky, like Feast Lake standing up on edge," his father said.

Aaron knew if it were dark, the clouds would be alive with lightning. He couldn't even hear their thunder, so he was sure they were far to the north, far beyond even the logging camps.

"If you start guiding, you'll never come logging," Nils had said.

No: he was doing all right. He'd made mistakes, but he'd given them chances at fish. And he'd kept their life jackets on. And he'd come out on Feast Lake. He was showing his father that he could handle things.

The boat was moving up even with the red and tan docks. But this was the best chance for getting to the timber he'd ever had, and a muskie would make it better. Aaron didn't slow the boat down. He kept angling it and rocking it over another shoving wave; another shoving wave; another shoving wave. . . . Like the men, he was begging for luck, and beggars had to keep moving.

21

HE SPED AGAIN *through the water. The swift, thin attack had missed and sank, but it had ended his curiosity and left him very alert.*

A small fish flickered to one side of him and reminded him sharply of hunger; he bent his rush and snatched it. But the fish bit him back and clung to his jaw, and he couldn't swallow or spit it; so he raced away, but it clung, prickling.

On Feast Lake City Dock a young boy fishing for perch barely held onto his fishing rod but could not stop his line whirring out from his reel.

"Daddy! Daddy!" he shouted.

The dark-haired man near him grabbed the rod as the last of the line unwound—the rod lurched, the man's grip tightened, the line snapped and disappeared.

"What was it?" the father gasped.

The muskie went toward the bottom. The crushed minnow clung and pestered in his mouth.

He swirled; the minnow clung. Its thin, trailing tail curled up to him; he bit at it, cutting the line off short.

He swirled again, and somersaulted. The shredded minnow fell away, but something tiny kept biting at his jaw.

He swirled again and looped over again and shook, and something hard and thin and sharp came loose in his mouth. He spit it out. Successful and free he raced to the surface and upended, his tail forking into the air and striking a hard, clear splash.

"Look!" the young boy shouted.

"Why didn't you take *my* bait!" his father yelled.

22

"KEEP YOUR LINES APART; we're turning," Aaron called out into the hot blow of the wind.

The men had grown weary, wanting to troll. Now they were sitting with all their lines stretching back past his shoulders, and they were staring back past him, too, and twitching the lines, trying to give their baits faked life.

The shoreline was cluttered now with the empty anchored boats and small docks of the Feast Lake townspeople, and the City Dock was growing longer and blacker ahead of him; he began turning to go out around it.

Beyond the Dock the beaches began, and the wind was whipping the shallow, sandy water into thick waves. He had to keep going farther out in order to have depth enough for fishing, and he had to keep tacking left and right to keep from being rocked too much broadside. But water kept splashing in over the sides.

The tall thin man's voice rose up husky and clear. "We're just getting another boat ride," he complained to the others.

"Are there really any muskies here?" the soft green man whined faintly up front. "You'd think we'd have seen them."

"They're here, all right!" the short thin man spoke out loudly, and Aaron saw the man wink at him.

Aaron didn't wink back. He worked harder at the motor. It was only a short distance on to the sawmill now, and he had to keep them fishing.

The water deepened near the sawmill, and he began angling back toward shore. The wind began to carry faintly, then stronger and stronger, the spicy smell of fresh timber. He heard the energetic high-and-low singing of the saws, and he couldn't resist pointing and saying loudly, "Someday I'm going to catch fish like those."

The men looked.

Smoke from the rusty, humped sawdust burner was leaping out and running flat with the wind. But Aaron was pointing lower, toward the heavy, new-cut logs that were slowly being herded by men atop them toward big hooks, which lifted them one by one into the sawmill. The logs were held in by a floating fence of other logs, chained together elephant-parade fashion.

"You really think there're muskies in here that big?" the short thin man asked, his lips smiling thinly.

"I mean *logs*," Aaron said. "I'm going to work with the timber."

The short thin man's grin ended. "Hey, how much machinery do they need to bring in those eighty dollar loads?" he spoke out.

"A tractor or horse, something to snake the logs out of the brush, then a truck," Aaron answered.

"And power saws?"

"Sure," Aaron told him. "Only Bob Dover, that's one of the men, says it's Mr. Carlson's singing that really brings the trees down. And Mr. Carlson says he's going to pour beef blood on the trees so the mosquitoes'll chew them down. There're laughs like that—"

"They have a truck for each man or what?" the short thin man interrupted.

"It takes two men to load a truck a day. They cost five thousand dollars."

"New or used?"

"Used—I think," said Aaron.

"What're you going to do, Bert, reel in and go logging?" The tall thin man's voice boomed.

"I'm a businessman. I've got to be interested in businesses," the short thin man called back over his

shoulder. "And this lad seems to know a lot about it."
To Aaron he said, "Maybe you could also guide me around the logging camps?"

"Sure!" Aaron said strongly. "How about tomorrow morning? Nils and I could find different people to tell you about everything."

"Nils?" asked the short thin man. His wide face was jutting forward, all creased with interest.

"Mr. Carlson's son. We're trying to spend our whole summers learning about timber."

"Then what?" The short thin man was looking even more intently at him.

"Then we're going to Montana, and Oregon, and Alaska. We'll be able to handle all kinds of logging."

"Then what?" The short thin man's face sparkled with interest.

"We'll go into business for ourselves, when we get big enough."

"Well, it's good to start young," the short thin man agreed. Then he sat back, still holding his fishing rod out low from his lap, but not waggling it, for he kept looking at Aaron. Then he said, "You'd be willing to work all your summers to learn about logging?"

"Sure!" said Aaron.

The short thin man's face came forward again; his eyes were very sharp and clear in their wide slits. "You gotta chance to fish muskies all summer all your life, and you're going to run off to be a—a tree butcher? You're a crazy kid."

Aaron held his tongue and locked his thoughts safe and silent inside himself. He felt how hoarse he was from the loud talking. He sank back weary and alone into the noise of the wind and the busy muttering of the small motor, and kept wrestling with the swaying and splashing of the boat.

The sound and scents of the sawmill faded out behind as he reached Feast Lake's eastern shore. He was farther from home than he'd been at Mink Bay, but he hadn't planned on coming here at all.

Now there was still no muskie, and the sun was more than halfway down the sky. The huge cloud banks were standing all across the water's northern rim, and he saw the vast middle of the lake everywhere blown into sharp, tossing peaks of water and choking white foam.

Yet he kept telling himself that there was still time; he wanted to get to go to the timber, and he'd keep these men fishing until it was dark enough that— anyway there were marshy coves and houses enough along this eastern shore to head into if he had to. He turned northward. He relaxed a little, for it was easier being pointed with the waves than across them.

He heard a drumming begin from among the shoreline trees behind him, and he looked around, hearing the sound rapidly become louder. Nearer and nearer out from the southern shore he saw waved-up water beginning to glitter and flake, and with a wallop the wind gust swept and sprayed over him; it kept gushing widely toward the storm clouds and he grasped heavily onto the small motor's steering-arm because around him the waves swiftly began rising up harder and taller.

Overhead the sky was dark blue.

23

ONCE AGAIN HE *had calmed. He was more alert. He felt his hunger more strongly inside him. He sensed the changing weather above him suddenly changing more. Change was uncertain. His hunger sharpened more. He ignored the dim hurting now in his mouth; it interfered with nothing. He swam smoothly, his long, stout body needing scarcely a ripple to produce its speed; briefly his stripes were a dark flickering in the dim, green water, and then he was in a new weed bed. His hunger now was urgent. He stayed here and waited, restless and impatient, but barely moving.*

Somewhere in the sandy mud near him a dragonfly nymph was struggling about, and a few small bubbles sparkled upward. The muskie started to follow the bubbles, then sank back and kept watching the misty glitter of green daylight constantly brightening and shadowing, flickering unpredictably around him as the waves on the surface grew stronger. He saw the slightest flicker of a movement that was steady, rhythmic. A small shape was moving among the weeds, stroking toward shore; the muskie rushed.

He swept over the frog like a hurricane. His jaws snapped and crushed. He sank to the bottom again; held still, and swallowed the frog. It was not enough. He ached for more. He lay still.

And fish came, their shapes blurred and constantly ballooning and shrinking in the unsteady light that was getting through the thick waves, but they moved in straight darts, like the frog.

The muskie flashed upwards, streaking between the one fish in the lead and the two behind; he struck, and at once he saw and tasted strangeness that wasn't food, and jerked away. Something jerked him back. He swirled viciously. The thing hurt and held him. He heaved tail up, wild at the slightest pull on his freedom, and thrashed toward the bottom. He shook. The thing in his mouth kept dragging back on him.

He cut upward and raced toward the surface. His long, thick body tensed and snapped, and he burst through, went straight upward, free of the water into glaring, dry light, and snapped again before he bent downward and splashed in headfirst.

24

"IS HE STILL ON?" the short thin man shouted.

The soft green man was hunched up and bent over, and his shoulders and hands were shaking as he clung to his fishing rod. "I can feel him! It's a muskie—I saw him!"

"Snug but loose! Keep it snug but loose. Don't let him snap it!" the tall thin man was bellowing.

The boat kept rocking them all among the rising waves that were tumbling and splashing from behind it. Aaron had throttled down and was trying to keep the boat steady, taking the blows the steering-arm would suddenly swing against his chest. He heard the small motor still whining and snorting as it churned shallow and deep. He saw the glistening fishing lines that stretched past him jerking violently as the two thin men reeled in, while the soft green man's line went snapping smoothly outward. Then it went slack.

"He's coming back! Reel in!" Aaron shouted.

A gunshot crash of water, and the fish broke straight upward again, vibrating dark and silver in the sunlight; its big fins glowed blood red as it bent. "Muskie!" Aaron yelled, and heard their voices echo him. It dove under coming toward the boat.

"I'm reeling, I'm reeling!" the soft green man wailed.

Aaron saw the line curling loosely toward the boat faster than it was being wound. He throttled the boat faster. The speed brought the two other baits bouncing and skipping to the surface, the orange plug and the hairy, bright-nosed bucktail chasing close together through the wave froth.

The muskie exploded in front of the baits, almost in Aaron's face, dancing on its tail just an arm's reach away. Aaron saw the soft green man's bait beneath the jaws as the muskie plunged downward, across the other lines. The two free baits flipped up and collided within the muskie's splash, as Aaron spun off the throttle. But the boat had no brakes; all the lines snapped taut at once.

"Let out! *All of you!*" Aaron shouted, for the other baits were all wound together in the soft green man's line. When he shouted, the men, who'd suddenly stiffened, openmouthed, let their reels unwind. The

baits had already disappeared below the waves and now went under the boat; the men all shifted to one side, holding their bent rods far out over the water to keep the lines from being cut against the boat's edges, and the boat started to roll under them.

Aaron fought back. He throttled and hauled on the small steering-arm. His tired muscles felt like glass, but he changed the roll into a turnaround; and the boat's stout bow, aiming back toward the south shore, began bobbing and crashing against the waves, splitting them as they came.

25

A BIG SHADOW *went over him; he felt something stronger tug at him and saw a hairy shape charging down after him; he spun about to fight, but he had bitten down viciously on the thing in his mouth and now his jaws were held shut by three more of its hooked teeth. He turned and aimed for the shelter of the weeds and had to drive deeper and toward shore for them. He flurried in among the first weeds he reached and then stopped, his stripes blending, his fins working tensely. He found the tugging pressure had gone away and there was just the sharp, light weight holding his mouth.*

The hairy shape, with spiny feet now hanging from it, waited limply a short distance to the side and above him; a stiff dark line went upward through it from a weedstalk. A thin silver tail stretched from the thing in his mouth to the weedstalk. But nothing moved. Impatiently he attacked the thing in his mouth: twisting tightly, shaking, crashing down against the mud. The mud clouded up, and his jaw sprang open as two of the hooks twitched loose; he darted to be free of the blurring mud, but the thing at his mouth jerked him to a stop and something shook more mud loose around him. Blinded, he tried to rush higher; again his jaw was jerked sharply back down, only this time the caught weed was jerked loose and jumped upward in a suddenly large mud cloud. In blind panic the muskie fought toward the surface again, pulling the weed and the hairy animal behind him, all dragging against the two points biting deeper through his jaw. So he strained to swim faster, and tensed as he neared the brightness and smashed upward; again he escaped the water. His tail flung up as he flew clear, but he felt his head weighted back, off balance. He struck down against the surface flat on his side.

Now his breathing came hard. His muscles felt softened. But there was no more pressure on him. There was only the meaningless pester in his mouth, and its thin silver tail and a weed lying loosely in front of him. Half-stunned, he floated on the surface, watching, and resting.

26

"HE'S WORN OUT. We're going to get him!" The soft green man was panting.

"Stay alert! Keep it snug! Keep together!" The tall thin man's voice was commanding. Both thin men's baits were still tangled and looped tight in the soft green man's line.

The waves kept beating and spraying against the bow, shoving the boat hard against Aaron's grasp. He'd forced himself to slow the motor, trying to keep the boat just pointed steady. He shouldn't move shoreward now; he should get far out from the weeds. But at the same time, he didn't want to be pushed too far out.

The men had all gotten back from the boat's edge and were balancing half-kneeling and half-standing, riding their thwarts as if they were saddles, trying to wind each reel at the same speed.

"Keep him coming," the short thin man called out, "but loose. One line gets too tight, and he'll break free."

"No! Loose will tangle it worse. And the hooks'll cut the line," bellowed the tall thin man.

"Keep watching him. Be ready—please!" the soft green man cried out.

"Keep it snug! Stay together!" shouted the tall thin man.

The muskie lengthened and thickened, coming toward them, visible now and then at the top of a wave, a vaguely striped dark glow within the water. A muskie weed was washing around ahead of the fish. Ahead of the weed the deer hair of the tall thin man's bait was draped like a soggy blanket around the bright orange of the short thin man's wooden plug. The water foamed around them. Everything was drawing closer.

Aaron switched the motor off completely to stop the propeller blades. When the motor stopped, the rush of the warm wind and cold waves seemed to get louder. The boat immediately swung broadside and began to skid and roll sideways among the waves, moving out into the lake.

The swing put the muskie behind the boat; the lines passed over Aaron's shoulder again.

"I can't see it now! I can't see it!" the soft green

man yelled. "All I can feel on my line is the baits."

"He's still coming," the short thin man yelled back.

"Keep it snug! Keep together!" bellowed the tall thin man.

"You'll feel him jump when he reaches the boat," Aaron warned.

"He's still too far out to net." The short thin man said. "We can't get him close with all this tangle."

"Let's cut something or tie *something!*" shouted the soft green man.

But they just kept drawing the muskie nearer. It floated toward them, staying in the tops of the waves, rising and lowering, but without skidding or rolling.

Aaron loosened the net again. They'd have to use the net. The gaff hook had a shorter handle and had to hit too narrow a target beneath the jaws.

Aaron looked and saw the soft green man balancing and swaying, clutching his fishing rod the way baby raccoons clung to branches that were being shaken. But it was the soft green man's catch. He had the right to try and net it.

Aaron gritted his teeth and called out, "Here, I'll pass the net up front."

"No! I can't let go my reel yet!" the soft green man screamed.

"One of us lets go of a reel, and that fish ruins us," the short thin man hissed loudly.

"You said *you'd* net one right. Now do it!" The tall thin man's voice roared. Aaron felt his face get hotter than the wind. The water splashing in on him felt icy.

He pushed the small motor's steering-arm to one side, then pressed a hip against it and tried to set one knee firmly down on his thwart, trying to brace himself so he could lower the net slowly in spite of the swaying. He was already guessing the muskie close to fifteen pounds; and he knew that if he got it hanging at the end of the long net handle, that weight would pull down like fifty.

He steadied the net against the gunwale as he watched the men's lines being drawn closer; the tangled baits came past the motor and along the boatside below him. Then they were raised out of the water, the three lines separating above the tangle, each line bending toward the tip of the rod it came from. In a moment the lines were spread tight and could be reeled no further.

The muskie still lay a long reach out, almost a part of the water itself, as if the gigantic lake had two tiny eyes and a flat mouth the size of a book, as if the eyes and mouth and brains of the lake were right there in front of the boat.

The tall thin man, balancing only by gripping his thwart between his knees, and trying to manage his reel in one hand, began easing a long thin arm out to reach the line at the tip of his rod, to pull the line in closer with that other hand, the way you could easily pull in a small perch.

Aaron started to stretch out and pull the line in for him with the frame of the net, but then decided not to interfere, and instead he slowly lowered the netting to the water.

With a smash of spray the men were frantically grappling at their whirring reels; the fish and the baits were gone.

27

HE SPIRALED DOWNWARD, *still the meaningless dead weight tugging deeply in his jaw. Its thin silver tail kept wrapping around him and he snapped at it; the metal leader bent and burnt between his teeth but didn't break. Suddenly he stopped. The hairy shape that was still following him stopped and went limp again, and the weed, too. He was becoming more bewildered than alarmed by them. He was starting to feel more tired than alarmed. He wanted to rest and watch again. But he was chary of going back toward the weeds right there.*

The sharp thing in his mouth jerked upward and kept pulling. He pulled against it. The thing in his mouth wouldn't stop dragging at him. He got angry, wanting to go where he wanted, and kept trying to swim backwards against it. It became too tiring. He gave in, let himself be towed upward, resting, watching, as he rose.

Now he was following the limp shapes that had followed him; he went back up into the glistening bright water. Just below the foaming surface he again gently swam forward. That eased the tugging on his jaw.

28

AARON SAW THE GHOST growing again in the water. The muskie seemed to be returning purposefully, coming from straight out at the side now, its dark, winkless eyes staring like gun barrels.

The torn weed was still washing around ahead of the muskie. In front of the weed the colorful foam of tangled baits came bobbing once more to the boat's edge; the baits were lifted.

Aaron's breath tightened and came harder. He began quickly and constantly making little shifts of position, trying to be sure he was braced.

The fishing lines again spread apart and stopped rigidly, holding the tangle again suspended in mid-air; the muskie stayed quietly floating up and down in the rough waves. Aaron started easing out the net; he stared down at the fish's staring eyes, round and dark, watchful and hostile. Aaron felt very alone and friendless.

He kept waiting for something to start. The boat kept rocking him and slamming among the waves. Aaron noticed that this time the tall thin man seemed to be just waiting, too; glaring down toward the fish. He saw that the soft green man's face was almost purple with blood veins puffing out like thick string. While close beside Aaron the short thin man crouched, watching, with only one movement—a thumb rubbing slowly round and round his reel.

But Aaron could not wait. As he swayed with the boat, he leaned the net out and eased it down across the soft green man's single line, beneath the tangled baits. He made the rim touch just above the glimmer of the steel leader: the line was breakable there but it would vibrate less than the steel. Slowly he pulled back, and the line curved tightly around the net's rim as the weed, and then the muskie, slowly followed his pull, closer to the boat, and then the weed was slapping against the boat. The muskie rode up close to the boat with the next wave, and sank away as the wave dropped. And rose again, and sank.

Aaron eased the net off the line, sliding it into the water, waiting the rhythm of the waves, and then quickly he swept the net toward the muskie and pried up; the waves burst all apart. His arms yanked at his shoulders, but he forced his hands to squeeze and wouldn't let go. He felt himself rising, saw the boat's edge slide away beneath his knees, saw nothing but waves leaping beneath him. He stayed weightless above them, his clamped hands jolting—then he realized he was being held, too. He felt the squeeze of something—an arm—around the padding of his life jacket and saw the blur of the short thin man's hair close behind his head, and he saw the tall thin man's hands gripping the heaving net out in front of his own.

Aaron got his knees bent, got them quickly back down below the gunwale; and bracing, but with the short thin man still supporting him, he anchored and pivoted the net handle as the tall thin man, with long legs shoved wide, lifted the handle up. The net came up deeply sagging and wildly jolting from side to side. They swung it inward and dropped it on the floor.

The muskie thrashed and struck sharply around their ankles. They kept their feet stamping and dancing away from the teeth and tried also to work with their hands. The soft green man's bait was tossed loose, clear of the net. The short thin man finally got the net rim beneath his sneakers, trying to press the muskie down; Aaron had snapped loose the gaff; the tall thin man reached and took it, swung it up and down like a hammer, and the thrashing stopped.

The muskie stirred just slightly. Its fins were bright

scarlet. It lay nearly a yard long on the bottom of the boat, rocking easily among the water that was still splashing over the gunwales; and in that water its body was brightening, too, and began shining deep green and silver, like a huge, magic coal that might shatter into ashes if someone tried to touch it.

The soft green man let loose of his rod. The excitement in his face was less frightening than the tenseness earlier had been. Suddenly he shouted out: "We've got him!"

"We've got a muskie!" Aaron yelled, too.

"Ho-de-HAY!" the short thin man yowled, and his mouth closed only to a wide, white grin.

"The world's leaping treasure!" the tall thin man roared, as he settled down and hung onto the rocking gunwales again, for the boat had been steadily drifting further from shore and was rocking steeply.

"Glory be, glory be!" the soft green man repeated. "The last day. Almost the very last hour!"

"Gentlemen, we're successes," proclaimed the tall thin man.

Aaron kept still now. He had a muskie in the boat to show to his father. He felt so full of success that words were bothersome.

"I'll tell you we earned this one," the short thin man spoke out. "Let's get him on the stringer."

"Look out!" screamed the soft green man. "Quick! There!"

Startled back to alertness, and so half off-balance again, Aaron looked; something huge and stiff and dark heaved near them among the waves. It floundered forward and heaved and rolled closer, then lunged onward just ahead of the boat's rocking bow. It lifted thickly and struck on past. Then Aaron saw another shape approaching, thick and solid, longer than the boat. Beyond that there was another; off to the sides still more.

29

"LOGS!" GASPED the short thin man.

"The wind's smashed them through that corral," the tall thin man roared.

"They'll smash us!" cried the soft green man.

Aaron had quickly turned and taken hold of the big motor's starter. He yanked it. The motor gunned; then it whirred in idleness as Aaron tried to stand up high to see where the logs were.

"Why the devil don't they build their stuff right?" the short thin man shouted angrily.

"Worry about that on shore! Let's get going!" the tall thin man shouted loudly.

Aaron had to sit back down and hang on. He had seen many more logs coming—just brief darknesses amid the foam and tumble of the waves; they seemed to be guarding the south shore like huge hounds. And the east shore right here was all marsh.

"Come on! Clear out!" the short thin man shouted right in Aaron's face.

"Let's go! Hurry!" screamed the soft green man.

Go where? Aaron had to wonder.

Another log rose up nearby, long and low in the water like an arm from the lake bottom. It lunged on forward, moving faster than the boat. Sideways, the boat was a steady target for waves and logs both, and broadside to the waves was how they'd have to travel if he tried to get back westward to the Deer Walk.

Aaron knew he could head northward with the wind again and outrace all the logs. But that meant trying to go across the whole open length of the lake where the waves would be wild enough to snatch the boat over.

The marsh then was the quickest and safest place to head for—

"Let's go! Let's go! We'll be killed!" the soft green man was shrieking.

But they could never walk out through the marsh, and the wind might keep blowing late and his father would come out searching in his own guide boat, into the waves at night, and maybe not know of the logs, and with the flu.

Another log plunged by, its blunt ends rolling up, glistening and dripping, and crashing down. Aaron had barely seen it coming.

127

It'd serve him right for making me be here now,
Aaron thought—then bit back the thought and tried
quickly to rub out that he'd ever thought it. He
didn't mean it. Nothing like that. He had a muskie to
show. He just had to get going across to the Deer
Walk was all.

He noticed the short thin man shifting toward him,
the tall thin man, too; both men were glaring at him
as if they were going to try to take him away from
his seat by the motor.

Aaron shoved the gear lever into forward and
twisted the throttle; the big motor roared as its propeller bit against the water. He felt the boat move
under his control, turning westward. He felt the
watchful spirits crowd close about him. He clapped
one hand briefly over his eyes to show the men, to be
honest with them, that he was going to race almost
blindly.

The tall thin man peered back at Aaron, then
shouted something at the others; soon the two shorter
men were crouched up front, weighting down the
bow and bracing the tall thin man as he knelt up on
the front thwart with his shoulders and his long thin
face high and watchful.

Aaron saw the long thin arms jerking and pointing
at near logs; and he kept cutting the boat half across
the waves, running with them, over their foamy
ridges, then veering about in a low trough and jam-

ming back at an angle into the next few, now veering again, speeding and turning according to the waves and the warnings, but always zigzagging to keep from getting rolled over broadside, and to make the boat a narrower target for any logs.

He saw the tall thin man's arms moving feverishly, and another log bobbed up like a floundering bull, crashing headlong through a wave just as he started the boat into it. Aaron swung the steering-arm and rapidly twisted the throttle back and forth. The boat dipped sideways, then skidded about, and he was traveling along beside the log, going faster than the log and the waves. He had to keep careering northward toward the bruised-looking storm clouds, riding up over ever bigger wave swells and splashing down between them, until he could no longer glimpse the log behind him; then in the quick bottom of another trough he swerved and cut across the log's path.

Abruptly he swerved again, back toward the Deer Walk, making the boat slam steadily against the wind and waves, and his thoughts were celebrating the escape he'd just made.

If the waves and logs were fast, he could go faster; if they were stronger, he was smarter.

A thin, swift-moving log suddenly shot from deep within a wave. There wasn't time or need for the tall thin man to signal. Aaron shoved at the steering-arm and throttle while the boat was sucked into a tailfirst

slide. It bounced off the side of the log, swung about, immediately began rocking and jolting as wave after wave kept striking it sideways; Aaron held onto the big motor to keep his balance; the motor whined high and steady, but would not control the boat. Suddenly Aaron guessed that its prop had been struck and something was broken. He grasped at the small motor; he nearly fell over yanking at its starter. His heart pounded with relief when he heard the small motor growl lightly but harshly and then begin muttering steadily. Aaron shoved it into gear, revved up the throttle, and tried to angle the boat into the waves.

The small motor chattered and growled, but the boat barely responded, still heaving up and shaking sideways with every rush of a wave. Aaron kept fighting to turn it, and every moment he braced to be tipped over. He got the boat canted enough that a wave slapped it around, pointing it southward, and the weighted bow dipped forward and slid smoothly and sluggishly down the back of the wave. Then the bow barely lifted and plowed straight into the next wave, and Aaron felt part of his legs grow cold. He saw water sloshing around in the boat. He saw where the log had cracked open part of the boat's side, and he knew why the boat acted so heavy, why it hadn't turned and hadn't tipped. Instead it could sink.

The bailing bucket was stowed right beneath his seat, yet he had no arm free and his voice could scarcely be heard. There was no need to shout, the men were already emptying their tackle boxes and were trying to bail with them.

30

HE LAY WAITING, *watching, in the shade of an over-hanging ledge, and protected on three sides by dead wood banks; yet he was rocking about in senseless, baffling ways, and chattering, growling sounds were always at him. His head ached tightly and harshly in a way he had never felt before. But there was fresher water moving steadily about him now, less deathly thick with the oily sourness that had been dripping around him.*

The change let him feel better, and he tried to attack the two live movements in front of him. Everything spun, and he felt sick. His muscles wouldn't work the way he wanted. He stopped. Never since long ago when he'd always stayed in the marsh had he been so constantly the weaker one.

He lay cautiously still, waiting and watching, let-

ting himself be rocked, and spreading and closing his gills, trying to pull through them as much of the fresh, soothing water as he could.

His color was growing a little paler, and low sunlight was flashing in on him.

31

THE MEN, MOVING up and down like strange pecking birds, kept bailing. Their actions, and the dazzling rows of foam constantly crashing and spraying about the bow, made it impossible for Aaron to see ahead clearly. No one was watching for logs; Aaron hoped they'd gotten far enough crosswind to be clear of the stampede. He just kept angling for the drooping sky, the pinkish-blue gap he could see in the southwestern shoreline. The water-loaded boat swayed and crashed against the waves; he steered hard to left and right. He saw the long dark shore line becoming larger.

Gradually the sky in the gap of the Deer Walk got wider around the bailing men. Through it the late sun, settling near the treetops, began to glare in Aaron's face.

Aaron had to work toward the shallow passage

while still being shaken about, dazzled by water and movements, and nearly blinded by light. He turned his squinting eyes more toward the edge of the steady, shadowed bulk of the trees on shore, but he also kept catching, against the sun's glare, the dark, flashing placard, wildly swinging on its wires in the hot wind. The placard slowly seemed to flutter higher and higher, till it was above the sun's glare. He watched it pass directly overhead, and right away the water grew calmer. The boat began moving with only gentle swayings. The men looked up and around; they were on Feather Bay.

Aaron could only grin.

The grin came back on the short thin man's face.

The soft green man yelled, "Hooray!"

"We've beat them!" boomed the tall thin man. "I hope their logs rot to splinters."

Aaron settled back, weary and half-relaxing, happily hearing the calm, steady throbbing of the small motor.

"Yes, gentlemen!" proclaimed the tall thin man, standing upright, panting and tired-looking, "now the captain rests at his labors; while we galley slaves must keep working." But then he smiled.

"I could bail that fish all the way to Chicago," puffed the soft green man happily.

Aaron said, "I could help if—"

"No! A mere flick of the wrist for us strong mus-

136

kie-catchers," claimed the tall thin man.

"Scoop away!" cheered the short thin man. "But I think it'd be easier just to swim to shore now—using our trusty life jackets."

"All right, let's vote on it," said the tall thin man.

"Please, let's stick to bailing!" said the soft green man.

Aaron suddenly realized the muskie wasn't there. He scurried about on his seat, panicked, and almost cried aloud in the moment before he found it floating stretched out in the partly shaded water beneath his thwart. Again he felt his heart thumping with relief. He felt all a-fluster. But he remembered the flag and got it out; and the soft green man happily stopped bailing long enough to take it and put it in its holder in the tip of the bow.

The sky above them was filling with the rosiness of evening. The small motor labored them along, slowly. The hot wind abruptly and quietly died away. Two paddling loons—big birds when you got near them—dove as the boat approached, and after several moments reappeared a long ways off. One of them began bugling; then repeated itself. Within moments a chill of icy air began dumping over everything from the north.

"Here comes the shivers," said Aaron.

"What?" the short thin man said, alerted and straightening up.

"The cold wind that's been fighting with the hot one, making the storm clouds. Feel it coming?"

"Southward," said the tall thin man. "Those big waves out there'll be turning back on each other, won't they? There'll be logs bobbing everywhere."

"We're safe here, aren't we?" said the soft green man.

"As long as you stick to bailing," said the tall thin man.

"We'll be in our channel soon," said Aaron.

He was already turning toward it. He kept the small motor muttering steadily through the channel, with enough speed and breeze to keep the flag fluttering. The sun went out of sight but sent gleaming rays of red and yellow back across the sky, coloring the high, distant tops of the thunderclouds behind them. The breeze got colder. The three tired fishermen, who would soon be paying out money to his father for everything that was happening to them, were still bailing out the boat.

They were halfway across Rennin's Bay when the bell started ringing in the cold air.

The three men sat up and stopped bailing. They simply sat up, very dignified and relaxed and proud-looking, while the water began seeping steadily above their ankles and the clang of the ringing grew slowly louder and closer. Aaron realized he'd never heard the bell from out on the water before; there'd never been any clanging when he'd come in with his family. What was his father going to say now, he wondered. What would his father say *now?*

Aaron saw his mother at the dock. And the two older people who'd been boat riding the evening before, and three others who'd also come to stay at the Inn early in the season. And several neighbors who must have hurried through the shore line woods at the sounding of the bell.

He guided the boat toward the dock. The proudly smiling men weren't bailing, and the boat was moving very deep in the calm water, already a third full of water. In the water about his legs, the muskie was still being constantly washed and cooled, and looked fresh and almost alive.

Voices began leaping out from the dock: "Who caught it?" "What's happened?" "Where is it?" "With what?" "Where?" "How?" "What's happened?" "When?" "Let's see it!"

The short thin man bent to pick up the muskie and show them, but stopped and groped around the bottom of the boat for the stringer he'd never attached. He found it, opened one of the large, stiff pins, and reached under Aaron's thwart and poked it through the wide skin of the fish's jaw. With a slam like a broken drum, the muskie shot out and upward; and the short thin man jerked upward. The muskie quivered in mid-air as the short thin man's feet dragged in the boat's water and he stumbled sideways and the back of his knees hit the gunwale. The muskie splashed straight back down in the boat as the short thin man sat swiftly down outside it.

The short thin man was up instantly, waist-deep in muddy harbor water and floundering back to the boat. But Aaron and the other men were after the muskie. It was darting back and forth beneath the thwarts, the bronze stringer pins trailing from its mouth like flame. The soft green man yelped as he missed grabbing the stringer and the muskie struck and ripped his trouser cuff and the flashing tail sliced sharply against his shin.

"The net!" the tall thin man bellowed.

Aaron grabbed the net.

The tall thin man suddenly reached for the gaff that was stuck near him.

The short thin man in the harbor caught hold of the gunwale and tried to haul himself back in. The muskie leaped again. Aaron swung the net. The net jolted from his hands as the swinging gaff struck it and lurched him toward the low side that the short thin man was leaning on. Aaron's weight made the boat tip further so that the tall thin man, off balance, too, and then the soft green man all slid to the side and the gunwale dipped below the water. The boat rolled up and there was no way to stand—Aaron watched the dark water rise up and felt it smash

around him; he beat about to get his feet under him. The boat had settled back, very deep in the water.

"He's still in the boat! He's still in the boat!" Aaron heard voices screaming from the dock.

He plunged at the boat with the men. The muskie crashed upward again, shook and danced against the sky, and came rainbowing over and hit among them. Then it flickered down and away, stringer and all, into darkness.

"*Why didn't you put on the stringer? Before! Before, before!*" the soft green man was suddenly shouting.

"You started yelling about those logs," the short thin man shouted back.

Aaron was too angry to care. He fought his way across the sticky bottom. Several people tried to help him, but he shook them off and heaved himself up onto the dock. There he found the tall thin man already standing and dripping, and he heard people all around him crying out all kinds of talk. His mother hurried beside him, but Aaron was too furious to stand still and stalked away from her. He met his father coming down off the path from the bell poles, bundled up in jackets, his face nearly hidden by a big scarf.

"Man, oh man!" his father said, with a raw voice that was straining to be loud enough. "This is the first chance I've ever had to ring my own bell."

"Well, you've wasted it," Aaron snapped loudly.

"What?" said his father. "Why?"

"It got away."

"*What* did?"

"The muskie. It jumped out."

"How? Out of what?"

"Out of the boat."

"When— Out of what boat?"

"That boat right there," said Aaron, spinning around and pointing sharply, but there was no guide boat to be seen. "The boat's down there. You can't see it. It's sunk," said Aaron.

"Sunk! You sunk the boat?"

"One of the logs cracked it."

"Which logs?"

"Oh you should have seen it, Mr. Rennin!" A lady who was one of the three new guests came rushing up. "It was a burst of shining colors! It leaped so smoothly, so powerfully!"

"A log leaped?"

"Not a log, Mr. Rennin. The muskie. The muskie these people brought back. Oh, I know I ought—"

"All you ever did was scream like a stuck pig over those logs!" The short thin man was climbing onto the dock, still arguing back at the soft green man behind him.

"If you were so calm then, why didn't you get the stringer on?" The soft green man's face was purplish again beneath his water-plastered hair.

"What a shame!" said someone.

"What a sight!" said another.

"Oh, but now the poor thing will get caught up and die with that stringer on!" the lady from the cabins exclaimed.

"I never even got the pin hooked. It'll shake it," the short thin man said to her as he pounced up beside them, his baggy clothing heavy and clinging and dark with mud and wet. "Don't worry about that."

"Don't worry about a thing, Mr. Brig," the tall thin man's voice crackled icily as he stepped close to them. "We always bathe, clothes and all this way, right after a hard week's work, Mr. Brig. And we always let our best fish go, when our guides don't get them stringered. It was all for cleanliness and kindness, everything. Everything happened just as planned."

"It was my catch," the soft green man said, talking to the people who'd just helped him onto the dock. "Then suddenly everybody else was hooked to it. I never felt that muskie again till it bit me." He bent over and began knotting a handkerchief around a bloody spot on his leg.

"We didn't catch a single thing," the tall thin man kept speaking at Aaron's father, "till we'd gotten weed-bound, and almost run down by a speedboat, and been driven around and around two islands until we were dizzy and roasting under life jackets—"

"Actually, I was glad for all the protection I could get," the soft green man murmured.

"We hooked a muskie when we *finally* got on the big lake," said the tall thin man.

"In terrible big waves," said the soft green man.

"Way over beyond that mill," said the short thin man. "It took a pretty good kid to handle a boat in that water."

"And three good men to bail it out on the way back," said the tall thin man. "But first—"

Aaron watched his father's eyes gleam brighter and brighter in the darkening twilight as from voice to voice the story was made clear, with only the short thin man ever taking his part, only the short thin man making it sound as if he'd helped. Aaron kept almost joining in, but thinking he'd best wait his turn.

Several times his father coughed downward into one fist. Finally his father slammed the fist twice against his other hand and shook a little. His voice was thin as sand and cracking into coughs, but he was laughing: "Four fellas spend all day—bringing in a muskie and—right at the dock it—dumps them, sinks the boat and runs off—with the stringer. This's the funniest thing I've heard in years— That's a muskie for you!"

"Thank you very much," said the tall thin man, sharply. "We'll have him baked right away, and *you* can come join us tonight for supper."

"Me, I've eaten more excitement than I could have found anywhere," said the short thin man. "But I'm still hungrier than these mosquitoes. Brig, I'll help raise that boat right after I find *any* kind of supper."

"I don't know whether to laugh or cry," said the soft green man.

"Laugh—'cause no one'll ever believe what we saw," Aaron heard one of his neighbors say. "That's the funniest part. We'll all swear to this, but no one'll ever believe us."

"And they were almost killed!" exclaimed the lady from the cabins.

It seemed to Aaron that everybody began trying to talk with everybody else again, and they all began moving slowly off the dock, all of them hardly bothering to swat the mosquitoes.

"I'll remember that muskie leaping out of that boat, longer than I could have remembered cooking him." Aaron realized it was his mother who'd spoken close beside him.

Then his father's hand came light but solid on his shoulder.

His father laughed hoarsely above his scarf. Then he coughed, and coughed again, and said, "That's a muskie for you. He's the king."

32

WITH HIS LOG LOAD heavy behind him, Aaron drew in toward the sawmill; the weight of the log, the roaring of the motor were all evenly under his control. He would unhook the log wherever the millman shouted it was wanted, and he would start out again, easy as that.

He grinned to himself. It was funny that already he was hauling logs to the sawmill—he and the other boat people around Feast Lake who had come out on the roundup. It was Sunday morning and nearly twenty boats were working on the calm after-storm waters, dragging in loose logs before new winds again filled the lake with moving, half-sunken battering rams.

It was hard work—for the motors. The soaked logs floated deeply, and their blunt ends dragged hard in the water. The air about the lake was filled with the grinding and roaring of laboring motors, and the rush of boats going out for new loads.

This rush of wind and fast movement of searching was fun, even though the quiet logs were not hard to find. The north wind working through the night had eventually driven most of them into certain areas. But there were a few exceptions, and already he and the short thin man had had an interesting struggle getting the heavy chain around an almost hidden and weed-tangled log.

The short thin man was staying over a few days. He'd asked to come along this morning. "If it's part of the logging business, I want to see it," he'd said to Aaron; and now using his father's guide boat as a tug, they were already bringing in their third log.

"How many's this?" the short thin man shouted back at the millman.

"Twenty-five of 'em," was the other's shout.

They roared away, and then later slowly they returned, drawing another log, and called out their question.

"Forty of 'em," was the reply.

They raced away, and then gradually brought in the fifty-ninth log, and then gradually they brought in the seventy-first, and then gradually they brought in the eighty-sixth. It was midafternoon before the swift searches and slow drags were over; the air

emptied of the steady motor grindings, and all
ninety-two logs that had been swept loose were lying
like stiff dead bodies in the repaired corral. On Monday morning the saws would whine into them. Aaron
remembered that he would be in school again, looking out. And when he got home after school, he'd
have to help clean out the two motors that had sunk
and patch up Roger's guide boat. Unless Roger got
another. Then if he had to patch it, there'd be three
guide boats—

He steered home slowly, along the Feast Lake south shore, toward the Deer Walk.

Three loons and then two more went racing silently past overhead.

The short thin man pointed up. He said, "Better make like them, or we won't get up to the timber today."

"There isn't much time left anyway," said Aaron.

"It won't be dark till eight, and it's only about twenty miles up there, isn't it? There'd still be time to show me around where your friends live."

"I was sort of thinking—" Aaron pointed vaguely at the water around him. "You suppose that muskie would have come back this far by now?"

The short thin man shrugged. "Who knows what a fish will do?"

Aaron shifted on his thwart nervously. "I mean as long as we're here—and I'm going to be in school all week . . ."

The short thin man stared back at him. "What would we do if we hooked him? It took four of us to get him in the boat yesterday."

"I don't know. Well—we probably wouldn't catch anything anyway." Aaron reached behind to turn the throttle faster.

"If we did catch one, it might be small enough for us to handle," said the short thin man quickly.

"Maybe in this calm water we could handle a bigger one," said Aaron. "And I know another place to show you." He turned from the throttle and reached instead to start loosening the spare fishing rods his father always kept clamped in his guide boat. "It's called the Pasture, and it's kind of hard to find. But we'd have time today."

"It might be worth a try," said the short thin man. "As long as we're here."

"We're bound to hook another muskie someday," suggested Aaron.

"Well I'm in no hurry to quit the muskie business," said the short thin man. "But see here, I can go up to the timber on Monday, for all week. You're sure now you don't want to head home a-roaring?"

"I want to try to make that bell ring again."